An Echo of Ashes

Based on a true story.
The Great War and the Spanish Influenza
took them from the oil fields.

Ron Allen Ames

HISTORIUM PRESS U.S.A.

More on this book and the time it is based in at:
www.ronallenames.com

Hardcover ISBN: 978-1-962465-95-3
Paperback ISBN: 978-1-962465-96-0
Ebook ISBN: 978-1-962465-97-7

Published by Historium Press
a subsidiary of The Historical Fiction Co LLC

2025

DEDICATION

To the generation who faced World War One,
and the Spanish Influenza.

PREFACE

We are born into a specific moment in history and a particular place on Earth. These factors, whether advantageous or challenging, profoundly shape our lives, steering us down paths that, in another time and place, we might not have followed.

Before my father passed, he told me of a box in his house that he wanted me to have. My wife and I are keepers of the family genealogy and assumed that was why he was leaving it to us.

My mother had passed four years before my father. Their home sat empty for months after they were gone. When the family had healed enough to clear out the memories, we discovered the box. I recognized it as the one I had seen in my grandparents' home years before. We glanced through its contents of faded photographs, discolored letters, postcards, and yellowed newspaper clippings, before closing it again.

Months later, my cousin, Craig Ames, learned of what I had received. He contacted me and brought more information from his side of the family, including an old trombone. Whether it was my father's words that echoed in my mind, or that old trombone staring at me from the corner of the room, I was called to reopen the box. I rummaged through the contents again, realizing it was all from the years 1914 to 1919. The time of World War One and the Spanish Influenza Pandemic.

Then I spied a journal of my Great Uncle Earl's. As a child, I remembered seeing Earl's gravestone at Cheney Cemetery. Throughout my life my grandparents said little about the past, so all I knew of Earl was that my father had been named after him. I never understood when my Grandad Arthur once said of his older brother, "Earl was something more."

Through Earl's journals, I got to know him. His words describe his life of subsistence farming while operating oil leases, just as his family had for generations. He was also a gifted piano and trombone player. His musical brilliance had been nurtured by his musically inclined mother. His words also tell of a romance, hidden by time and now exposed after more than a century.

Earl's journals, along with the hundreds of other articles in the box, and what Craig had brought, were a window in time. I read on, becoming acquainted with the other family members of that era and the tribulations they faced in their time in history.

The information unveiled sparsely known local and national historic events, along with world issues dealing with the war and the pandemic.

Firsthand accounts of the home front filled page after page, along with letters from the western front of the Great War, and descriptions of the devastating consequences of the Spanish Influenza. There were pictures and letters about the US 13th Cavalry.

The rarely talked about oil business of that age is also chronicled in the words of laughter, love, and sorrow of a family of seven. How miraculous it was that this box had survived for so many years.

World War One and the Spanish Influenza Pandemic are two monumental events that changed the world. Though often chronicled separately, these two cataclysms occurred simultaneously in 1918. The people of this time endured hardship and loss. With their thoughts still echoing through the ashes of what had happened, many chose to rebuild their lives and seek new hope. This is but one of the countless stories from that chapter in history.

Written in story form to bring history alive, fiction surrounds actual events, personalizing the individuals, adding depth, and recreating the emotional impact of living in such a pivotal time.

Special thanks to:

Cathy; my loving wife, my advocate.

Craig Ames, for his research and shear enthusiasm.

Sandy Shreffler, for her inspiration and insight.

My family, and all of you who covered me over in prayers in my greatest time of need.

The doctors and nurses of UPMC who saved my life, allotting me the time to complete this work.

ACKNOWLEDGEMENT OF HISTORICAL REFERENCE SOURCES

1. Benson Memorial Library, Titusville, PA

   Jessica Hilburn, Executive Director, local historian, and author

2. Franklin Public Library, Franklin, PA

3. Oil City Library, Oil City, PA

   Judy Etzel, board member, local historian, and writer

4. Historic Drake Well Museum and Pithole City (covering the history of oil), www.drakewell.org

5. "How America Struggled to Bury the Dead During the 1918 Flu Pandemic" by Christopher Klein www.history.com

INTRODUCTION

Every story has its beginning. This one starts in 1914, in a nearby vicinity of an area called Goodwill Hill.

Like many rural places in Northwestern Pennsylvania, Goodwill Hill is known primarily to the local inhabitants and few others. Located in Southwest Township, Warren County, Goodwill Hill refers to a stretch of land that rises above the surrounding terrain. It is not far from the village of Enterprise, the borough of Pleasantville, and the city of Titusville. Until recently, only a secondary road sign displayed its name.

Goodwill Hill was settled in the late 1700s, at approximately the same time as the rest of the region. Through those early years, inhabitants primarily supported themselves as their forefathers had, by hunting, subsistence farming, and logging.

In 1859, near Titusville, oil was discovered. This started a new industry that created employment opportunities in much of the region, including Goodwill Hill.

The oil boom ushered in a time of great excess. A large population influx and oil exploration dramatically changed the landscape, causing wholesale destruction of native habitat. Along with uncontrolled hunting, the large game animals of deer, bear, and elk became exceedingly rare in Pennsylvania's woods. Rural hunters were primarily reduced to taking small game, such as squirrels and rabbits, to help feed their families. Laws were established in 1869 to regulate the taking of game and bounty animals. However, necessity and culture prompted some people to ignore these laws.

A broad spectrum of equipment was developed for the oil industry during this time. Some of these implements and the methods in which they were used brought more oil from the ground, but added to the danger of field production work.

By the 1870s the rush had dwindled, making way for oil production to develop into a sustainable industry, driven by some large companies and many small independent producers.

Relics of the industry's intemperate past scatter the landscape. Abandoned wells, pipelines, iron gears, train tracks, power engines, old tanks, and well jacks lay silently rusting away. Many structures — even the city of Pithole— were abandoned, leaving only rotting boards, broken glass, and slate roof tiles to proclaim what once was.

By the early 1900s, new forest growth was reclaiming some areas that had previously been clear cut for the well sites, oil derricks, and shanty buildings of the past.

Oil put new and old worlds on a collision course. A hodgepodge of automobiles and trucks now shared the same streets and roads as horses, buggies, and wagons. Electric trolley cars added to the mayhem.

The Compulsory School Law Act of 1901 was passed to standardize the education system in America. However, in rural areas, high absenteeism continued as the need for children to work at home, on the family farm at harvest time, and on oil leases, took priority over school. To alleviate this socio-economic problem, some schools split the day by creating a morning class and an afternoon class. This flexible schedule did help some.

World War I, the Great War, broke out in Europe in 1914. America officially entered the hostilities in April of 1917. The conscription of many young men into the military left a shortage of manpower to run the nation's vital agriculture industry. The U.S. Department of Labor created 'The United States Boys Working Reserve' to fill the vacancies. This controversial piece of legislation further disrupted the education of some students.

Among America's justifications for war was the unrestricted submarine attacks Germany carried out on any nation's merchant ships, including the United States. Other factors were the sinking of the passenger ship *Lusitania* and the "Zimmermann Telegram," a correspondence sent by Germany to Mexico proposing an alliance to fight the United States. The secret document was intercepted by

British intelligence and published in America's newspapers. This information, coupled with ongoing civil unrest in Mexico and the sporadic attacks on border towns and villages by outlaw bandits such as Pancho Villa, led the U.S. military to further strengthen its presence at the Mexican border.

An influenza outbreak, soon to become known as the Spanish Flu, began its treacherous reign in 1918 and took more American lives than the war ever would.

TABLE OF CONTENTS

CHAPTERS

This story is based on the journals of Earl Leslie Ames, family tales, research, and over 200 letters, postcards, and newspaper articles dating from 1914 to 1919. Some names have been changed.

Sojourner of time, when night ends the day and the certainty of tomorrow has yet to arrive, the ashes of yesterday are all that linger —echoing the story you left behind.

Ron Allen Ames

CHAPTER 1

The Hunt as the Nitro Magazine Explodes

November 21, 1914

Toe first, then heel, he cautiously stepped, trying to soften the crunch of the crusted snow beneath his boots. He stopped in his tracks—listening, gazing, searching for any movement, any color variation. Far off, the distant sound of a gathering breeze caught his attention. The gust passed over, gently shuffling the treetops and rustling the branches and dead oak leaves that still clung to last summer's perch. The chasing wind rumbled in his ears as he exhaled. His crystallized breath raced east. He turned in that direction. Facing the wind would obstruct his scent.

Resuming his quest, he traveled to a right-of-way that snaked across the landscape. The clear-cut strip enabled a jerk line, hung on the pendulum hooks of a long row of tripods, to slowly move back and forth. The connected steel rods of the jerk line supplied the push-pull movement to lift and lower the pump jacks. He raised his boot onto the line as it hesitated to reverse direction. He stepped to the other side, glancing about, watching for anything that might have been spooked by his sudden movement.

The far-off *puff, swoosh, swoosh, puff, swoosh, puff,* sound of a hit-and-miss engine of the central powerhouse echoed through the hills as it supplied the energy to make everything move. The squeaking of the moving jerk line behind him chimed in with the upstroke moan of the pump jack it was connected to. The sounds of a working oil lease created an eerie symphony so common to Northwestern Pennsylvania that it no longer spooked the wild creatures.

He ventured on until he noticed fresh tracks. He spied an old oil tank on a knoll, and walked to it. From there, he could watch over a grove of chestnut trees that had escaped the sawyer years ago. He pulled up the collar of his tattered coat, preparing for the chill he knew would come, cradled his rifle, and began the arduous watch.

Cold crept into his clothes as the high tree branches periodically danced to an intermittent breeze. He stood for what seemed like eternity until the shivering of his lanky stature became unbearable. He flipped his rifle to his arm, took one last look, and moved on.

He walked to the edge of a ridge and peered at the panorama. To his left, not far down the hill, he spied his brother Arthur sitting on a fallen tree.

Earl glanced up to the dismal, overcast sky. *Artie is wasting his time too. Not many squirrels will venture out on a day such as this.* Earl whistled the two-tone call of the chickadee. Arthur immediately turned to see who had interrupted the solitude. He spied his brother hand-signaling to move to the field below. Arthur grudgingly waved back as he reluctantly stood. His first step broke the forest's silence which had formed around him. He glanced about, then hunted on down the hill.

As the boys stepped from the tree line, Earl shouted, "There!" as a lone rabbit launched from its hiding place. The animal streaked through the clumps of dead grass and snow. Both hunters raised their guns, but neither had a shot.

"I saw where he went, Artie!" Earl hollered as he ran to a hole and stood. Arthur hurried over and circled around, pushing the grass with his boot until he found it.

"The back door is here," he stated as he pointed to a different hole. Arthur trotted over to Earl and knelt. He laid his 22-caliber rifle at his side and pulled off the sack that was strapped to his back. He reached inside and retrieved something small and furry.

"Get ready, Top," Arthur said (referring to his older brother who, being the first-born, was bestowed the nickname 'Top'.) Arthur looked the ferret in the eye and said, "All right, Buster, chase that rabbit out his back door." He lowered the little creature to the hole, and it scampered in.

A blue jay above them shrieked its alarming cry just as—*KABOOM*! A great concussion threw Arthur face-first into the hole. He angrily lifted himself while spouting, "You did not have to shoot that shotgun so close to me!" He flashed an irate gaze to Earl before noticing the stunned expression on his brother's face. It had not been gunfire. Arthur whirled around to see black smoke and bits of debris still falling from the sky.

"The nitroglycerin magazine!" Earl blurted out as he darted away. Arthur grabbed his rifle and followed.

The boys sprinted through the snow and protruding grass of the field, toward a homestead that stood in the distance. As they reached it, Arthur slowed at the sight of a group of frightened cattle huddled under a tree at the far corner of the fence. He noticed the front door of the house hanging open, its windows shattered— signs of a sudden tragedy.

"Uhh!" He tripped. Instinctively, he cradled his gun in his arms just before hitting the ground. His elbows and knees took the brunt of the fall.

Earl looked back and shouted, "Come on!"

Arthur crawled back to his feet, threw his rifle to his right hand, and began limping. The stinging pain barely slowed him down.

The boys were panting when they reached uprooted trees and broken branches that had been cast hundreds of feet from where they once stood. The two weaved through the destruction until they came to a crowd standing at the edge of a star-shaped crater. Their heavy breathing could not overshadow the shock they saw and felt. People were overcome with grief. Some were crying while others stood expressionless, like the huddled cattle.

Where the Adam Cupler Torpedo Company building had stood was a giant hole that contained a few splintered, smoldering boards, some broken bricks, and a few other pieces of wreckage. A couple of strands of fabric draped distant limbs that had not been ripped off by the blast. Sporadic splashes of blood, a few chunks of flesh, and a couple of broken bones, unrecognizable as either human or animal, lay alongside a piece of wagon wheel. There was nothing left.

Suddenly, the sound of a buckboard and team of horses halting caught everyone's attention. A man jumped from the rig and ran through the crowd, ranting, "My God! Windows are busted everywhere down the road! One house is pushed clear off its foundation!" The man shook his head as he mumbled, "Two hundred quarts of nitro . . . everything is gone." Reality crept in as he spotted the blood. His voice crackled, "I just sent him to load the shot."

The man pulled off his hat and dropped to his knees. With his hands over his face, he began to sob. A woman pushed through the crowd and knelt by the weeping man, consoling him as whispers speculated that the victim was Dick Gillen, a shooter from Titusville who worked for the company. Suddenly, through his tears, the man shouted, "It was Ralph!"

People gasped. Everyone in the local oil business knew Ralph Tubbs, one of the best moonlighters around. But that was years before. Ralph was now the person whom most companies turned to when they needed a shooter. But when nitroglycerin is involved, no matter how much experience one has handling it, anything can go wrong. Maybe Ralph had stumbled while carrying the quarts, one in each hand for balance as most shooters did. Perhaps the horse jerked the wagon. He could have dropped a quart while loading. Maybe it was just temperature change that caused the unstable mixture to explode. Whatever the reason, no one would ever know.

More people arrived just as John Litzinger stepped alongside Earl and Arthur: a stocky, dark-haired boy whom everyone called Jack. He had been a close friend of the Ames brothers since childhood. Jack stared at the disaster while saying, "I heard the explosion clear over at your grandmother's farm. I was helping Romey hoe out the barn when the dust shook out of the rafters. We both saw smoke in the sky, so Romey told me to take his horse and find out what happened."

Just then, the crowd parted, forming an avenue for a struggling old man with a crutch. His right pant leg was neatly folded and pinned just above the knee. The man limped up to the edge of the crater. He leaned on his crutch and stood silently, taking in the scene as his straggly gray beard moved slightly in the breeze. It was the old recluse, Mr. Regent. The Civil War had taken his leg and much of his soul.

"Looks like the war," the old man muttered as he lowered his head, turned, and made his way back through the crowd.

The silence broke as a model T ambulance pulled onto the scene, but all the drivers could do was hand burlap sacks to a few volunteers. The grim task of rummaging through the debris, trying to find what little was left of Ralph, was about to begin.

Arthur knelt to rub his still-stinging knee. That is when he noticed a red horse blanket on the ground at the edge of the crater. The cloth looked to be unblemished, an abnormality among the carnage. He picked it up as his mind pondered, *If this is what war looks like, then what leaves something escape unscathed? Does destiny choose what is to be spared? Or does fate foretell what is to be destroyed? Do the angels safeguard what is chosen?*

Arthur stood, still in deep thought, when Earl said, "There is nothing we can do here, Artie. We have chores, and then school. Let us go get your backpack. I do not know if we will ever find Buster. We may be putting a box trap out for him."

Arthur nodded and the two started back toward the field as images of the disaster continued searing into their minds. (This event was reported on the following morning in the Titusville Herald Newspaper, November 22, 1914, Page 1; and also, years later on November 15, 1984, Page 9, in an article titled 'Nitroglycerine Explosions,' in which Arthur Ames recalls.)

From that day forward, everyone referred to Dick, the man who had missed work that day, as 'Lucky,' a nickname that stayed with him the rest of his life. This catastrophe had been repeated in times past and, unfortunately, would repeat in the future.

Many local people worked in the dangerous oil industry. Some families had members in the business since its beginning. These people were the tool dressers, rig hands, drillers, pumpers, roustabouts, and shooters. They were not the ones who'd made the fortunes. They were the common folk who cleared the landings, manned the rigs, drilled the wells, built the pump jacks, laid the pipelines, and connected the jerk lines. They sent the crude to market for a paycheck.

Arthur and Earl were sons of this breed of worker. They had both started working in the oil fields at twelve years of age, and though it was dangerous; like their father, their grandfather, and his father before, it was the way of life they knew.

Mr. Regent's few words that day not only described the moment, but also would apply to a future peril. Those words would be remembered as the newspapers continued filling with stories of a Great War in Europe. Rumors circulated about the fear and excitement of America possibly becoming involved in that conflict, and what changes that entanglement might bring.

CHAPTER 2
The Girl with the Silver-Blue Eyes

December 1916, 2 years later

His eyes laggardly opened to the predawn light. The sight of newspaper pages pasted to the walls greeted him once more. Those pages had been put there to ward off the fiendish drafts that crept through the old, double-boarded farmhouse walls.

It was colder than usual. The wood stove must have burned down to nothing in the night. Earl crawled from his bed wearing only his union suit (one-piece long underwear). His thin, tall body shivered as he made his way to the stove, grabbed the poker, opened the door, and stoked the ashes. The sparkling glow of a few hot coals appeared. He grabbed some kindling and strategically placed them before he gently blew until tiny flames sprouted. He slowly fed in larger wood until the fire rumbled up the stovepipe. Warmth began radiating through the house. He grabbed the pail of water he kept in case the hand pump froze and placed it on the top of the stove. Soon the water would be warm enough to wash with.

He cleaned up and dressed. As he tugged his celluloid comb through his thick, wavy, dark brown hair, his mind sorted the day's tasks. The horse needed to be hayed, the Cambridge lease needed pumping, and then school—and after that, music practice.

He pulled on his old red hood, slipped on his gumboots, grabbed his hat and gloves and stuffed the sack with a sandwich in it into his pocket before going out the door.

Earl walked to the barn. The hinges squeaked as he pulled open the door and stepped inside. He grabbed the pitchfork and speared a large clump of hay from a broken bale, then tossed it over the stall railing to an eagerly waiting bay mare. The horse snorted and shook its head while following the hay down. "I know I am late, but you knew I would be here to feed you." Earl gave the horse a pat on its mane. He took his pitchfork and broke the thin skim of ice that had formed at the edges of the water trough, then sat down on a hay bale and pulled his greasy coveralls over his clothes just as the mare looked up.

She seemed puzzled that Earl was not reaching for the saddle. He responded, "The Cambridge lease needs pumping today, Dolly. And yes, yes, I know that lame leg of yours is healed, but one more day of rest is not going to hurt anything." The mare kept staring at Earl as he said, "I will be back later." He flipped up his hood, pulled on his gloves, and went out the door. The horse moved to the stall wall and peered through the gaps between the planks, watching until Earl's silhouette disappeared into a squall of snowflakes.

Earl walked the snow-covered road to a narrow lane that led to an old, rough-cut lumber powerhouse. He moved the pipe that propped the door, pulled it open, and stepped into the dingy light. A Reid fifteen-horsepower engine sat cold and quiet in the center of the room. He closed the petcock on the block and opened the main water valve. He turned on the gas, struck a wooden match, and lit the hot tube. While it was heating, he grabbed the long-neck oil can from the windowsill and filled the oilers before lubricating other parts of the engine.

Soon, the hot tube was glowing. He grabbed the flywheel and turned it right to set the piston at the start position. He forced the wheel left, to suck in fuel. Then he pulled it back three-quarters to charge the main cylinder. The engine was ready. *Here we go.* He heaved the wheel left with all his might. The flywheel bounced back and made a complete revolution as the engine let out a loud *puff! swoosh!* The dual flywheels slowly rotated again and let out another *puff! swoosh! swoosh!* and then another, and another, as the engine came alive. Earl adjusted the gas valve until the engine chugged up to full speed. He let everything warm a bit before squeezing the lock on the long clutch lever and pulling it toward him.

The clutch engaged as the canvas belt let out a squeal when it momentarily slipped on the flat pulleys. The noise rose as the eccentric gear began to rotate, pushing and pulling the jerk lines that were attached to it, and the wells began to pump.

The whirring sounds of the running machinery told Earl that everything was fine. It was time to follow the jerk lines to the wells; a task performed regularly, to make sure nothing had come apart or broken.

Hours passed as he walked the lease, and he lost track of the time. Finally, he pulled his old cracked-face watch from his pocket and looked. *Oh no!* It was late. He immediately ran back to the plant and shut it down before running home. He threw off his coveralls, grabbed his books, and raced through the snow to school.

Winded, he trudged up the steps, down the hall, and opened the classroom door. Miss Chelmadine gave him an annoyed look as he entered. "Second Class starts at noon, Mr. Ames."

"Yes, Miss Chelmadine."

Still panting, Earl took his seat as the teacher walked over. "Today is examination day. If you hurry, you can probably answer enough questions to get a passing grade." She handed the Latin test to Earl and walked away. He hastily rummaged for his pencil and started.

It seemed as if only minutes had passed before the teacher said, "Time is up, put down your pencils." Earl glanced up from his paper, and that is when he noticed the pretty girl with the flaxen hair sitting in the next row over. He had never seen her before. Suddenly, she glanced his way. Her silver-blue eyes showed like precious gems, piercing his soul. Earl stared back, stunned. His heart raced as his mind narrowed to just gazing at her. She seemed to be peering straight through him. Suddenly, she looked away.

Miss Chelmadine noticed the wordless interlude. As class let out, she escorted the girl over to Earl. "Mr. Ames, you missed the class introduction of our new student, Miss Lucile Lake. She just moved here."

Earl stood, dumbfounded, as the teacher walked away. He came to his senses and blurted out, "Earl . . . it is Earl."

Lucile impassively looked at the scruffy boy with tattered

clothes, messed hair, and dirty hands. "Hello," she snipped in an obligated manner.

"I . . ." was all Earl said before he was cut off.

"I am sorry, Mr. Ames, but I must excuse myself. I am expected home soon."

She immediately turned and walked to the line of garments hanging on the back wall. Her pleated brown dress gracefully flowed at her ankles with each step she took. She grabbed her coat and disappeared through the classroom door.

CHAPTER 3
The Pie Social

March 1917

The sun's rays, sparkling through leaf-barren trees, found Earl walking a trail along the edge of a ridge. The surrounding natural beauty usually caught his attention, but today his mind was wondering where the pretty girl with the piercing silver-blue eyes had gone. He had not seen her in weeks. *She must be taking first class instead of afternoon class. Did she move away?* His timidness had created a wall of reluctance to ask anyone about her, but he felt that he should somehow have bumped into her by now. That silent hope he held seemed to be drifting toward an unobtainable fantasy.

Reaching Well Number Seven, Earl touched his fingers to the polish rod. As the jack rose and dropped, abnormal vibrations caught his attention. The constant movement of the working box and the sucker rods may have worn a hole somewhere, or perhaps rust had claimed a place in the tubing. Earl grabbed a wrench from his pocket and loosened and slid up the stuffing box. He retrieved a round chunk of leather and a pocketknife from his other pocket, cutting a few triangles from the circle. He dropped the leather pieces down alongside the polish rod. Hopefully, they would lodge into any hole and the well could produce a bit longer. He snugged the stuffing box back in place, then stepped to the wooden separator tank and lifted the lid. The aroma of raw oil spewed stronger into the air as he peered inside. The green crude was still momentarily floating on the saltwater before sinking beneath it. But the flow was weak. The dribble spout on the side of the tank was splattering very little saltwater onto the ground. Although the amount that dripped was tiny, the fresh tracks of forest creatures indicated they were still coming to sip their needed salt. He closed the lid and moved to the next well.

Earl worked until the sun began to set. He walked home in the twilight and fed Dolly just as darkness overtook the evening. He entered his house and tossed a few pieces of firewood in the iron stove before lifting the chimney of an oil lamp and lighting it with a wooden match. As the lamp illuminated the room, his melancholy thoughts returned to that girl. He sat down on the piano bench just as the front door opened. It was his brother Arthur.

"Hello, Top! I trapped three weasels today," Arthur boasted. "One is white. You know he is a two-dollar bounty. Along with the other two, I got four dollars and forty cents coming. Well, no, I forgot that Justice of the Peace Langdon will take his twenty-five-cent fee for each one. But I will still have enough money left to pay you for that gun."

"Good, Artie," Earl replied, his mind still elsewhere.

"Well, you do not look like you are ready to go," Arthur spouted.

"Go where?"

"What do you mean, 'go where'? We are playing tonight for the church revival . . . remember? We are going to be late."

"I need a moment to clean up."

"Top, we do not have a moment. Throw on your clothes and let's go. Albo is hooking Dolly up to the wagon right now . . . I will get your horn." Arthur grabbed the trombone case from the corner as Earl commanded, "You make sure Albo is gentle with Dolly!"

"I will."

Earl hurriedly dressed and splashed on some cologne. He grabbed his coat and sheepskin gloves and ran out the door, hopping into the back of the wagon just as Albert flipped the reins and Dolly began to pull.

As they rode along, the only sounds echoing through the crisp evening air were the clip-clop of Dolly's hoofs and the hollow sound of wagon wheels on the dirt road. Earl was gazing at the star-filled sky when Arthur turned to him and asked, "Top, did you read about that 'Zimmerman Telegram' in the paper yesterday? Germany is trying to get Mexico to ally with them against us."

"I have not read the paper for a while," Earl replied.

"Well, I do not know where your head has been lately, but a lot of people think this is the last straw and President Wilson is going to declare war."

"I hope not," Earl replied.

"I hope so!" Albert spoke up. "I would join up in a minute to fight the Huns!"

"Albo, you are only sixteen," Earl replied. "Father and Mama would have to sign for you, and you know what that answer would be. Besides, we are talking about a war that has not yet been declared."

That statement ended the conversation until Arthur turned once more to Earl. "Top, do you remember what old Mr. Regent said that day when the nitro magazine exploded?"

"Yes," Earl replied.

The rest of the ride was quiet, and soon they were tying Dolly up to the post by the water trough outside the church. As the boys grabbed their horns, Earl lifted a bucket of oats from the back of the wagon and set it on the ground beside Dolly. "We will not be long, girl." The horse immediately dunked her head into the bucket and began to eat.

Walking through the back door of the church put the boys on stage with the other members of the band. As they unpacked their instruments and set up their music stands, Arthur remarked, "There must be a hundred people here."

Just then, Reverend Barber came up to the musicians and said, "Gentlemen, we appreciate the Pleasantville Band being the entertainment tonight. I will have you begin playing just after the opening introduction and prayer, and then I will signal for you to stop so I can give my sermon. Afterward, I will have you play one more song just before the pie social begins. Thank you for your service tonight."

The reverend then walked to the podium and said, "Hello, everyone. Please take your seats, the program is about to begin."

Soon the band was playing. Earl sat in the front row to the right, playing his trombone and making every note crisp and clear. Arthur sat next to him, playing his trumpet, Albert was on the far side with his coronet.

Earl glanced up from his music and there she was, setting a pie down on the table with the other pies. She never looked at the stage as she and an older woman squeezed into a pew. Arthur nudged Earl, who had stopped playing. That nudge stunned Earl back to reality too quickly and he blew a loud, off-key sound from his trombone. A few musicians and Lewis Watson, the director, threw a stunned glance at Earl. He regained his composure and continued to play.

Finally, the band finished. As his brothers watched in surprise, Earl hurriedly packed his trombone and darted out the back door. He startled Dolly as he ran past her and around the outside of the church. Uhhh! He slipped in the yard and fell. He clamored back to his feet and continued his trek while trying to wipe the mud from his clothes. Reaching the big front doors, he yanked them open and stumbled inside.

Reverend Barber spied Earl the moment the doors clanged shut. He glanced back to the stage, puzzled. How had that young man made it to the back of the congregation so fast? The reverend shrugged in amazement and continued, "Now, folks, I imagine everyone is starved from the sweet smell of all those pies. Well, we are going to start the bidding now, and the lucky winners get to share their pie with whomever the name is attached to it—or maybe you will not want to."

Everyone chuckled as the reverend shouted, "Amen!" He said, "Remember: your money goes to do God's work, so do not be stingy." Everyone chuckled again. The reverend picked up the first pie, held it high, and said, "Who will give me twenty-five cents for this pie?"

"I will," came from a man sitting to the left.

"Fifty cents," came from the right.

"Do I hear seventy-five cents?"

The bidding went on as Earl stared at the table. *Which pie is hers?* Arthur and Albert walked over to him. "We put the horns in the wagon," Arthur said. "You ready to go?"

Earl never heard them. He was still staring at the pies. Suddenly the pastor picked up another one.

That must be it!

The reverend held the pie up high, and before he could ask for a bid, Earl shouted, "One dollar!"

"My," the stunned reverend remarked, "you must really want this pie, son. Or maybe you are making up for that foul note you blew a little earlier?" The crowd giggled as Earl's face turned three shades of red. "Well, I doubt anyone is going to bid higher," the pastor said as he looked around. "Come up and get your pie."

Earl smiled as he quickly walked to the table and paid the man. He grabbed his pie and envelope as anticipation consumed his soul. He rushed back to where his brothers were, never noticing as the auction continued. He never heard Albert shout, "Seventy-five cents!" He never heard the pastor shout "Sold!" He never noticed Albert go up to get a pie. He was too consumed with ripping the envelope open.

"No name," Earl said out loud. Disheartened, he gazed at the empty envelope while consoling himself in the thought that it was not an insult—many girls and women put empty envelopes on their pies, not caring to eat with strangers. They were married, or they were shy. *Perhaps she is the shy type, but then, why did she come here tonight?*

Albert walked back to his two brothers and held his pie up. "We are going to eat good on the way home. Oh . . . and here is an envelope." Albert opened it and read, "Miss Lucile Lake."

"Give me that!" Earl stated as he grabbed for the pie, but Albert was too quick, and swung it from Earl's reach.

Earl instantly commanded, "Albo! Give me that pie!"

"No."

"Please, Albo. You can have this one."

"I do not like mincemeat."

"Okay, just give me your envelope. You can keep your pie."

"But, maybe I want to meet this girl."

"She is probably just some old spinster," Arthur injected.

Albert noticed the determination in Earl's eyes and decided it was time to barter. "Do I get to take Dolly for a ride?"

"All right," Earl reluctantly responded as he grabbed the envelope from Albert's hand. Earl immediately made his way to the pew where Lucile sat. He paused as she slowly looked up at this shabbily dressed man with muddy knees, whom she had been introduced to before.

Earl sensed she was staring at his shoddy clothes, but mustered his most charming voice and said, "Hello, again."

"The trombone player," Lucile replied in a demeaning manor as her mother looked on.

"Yes . . . I have your envelope, and am hoping you might share this pie with me."

Lucile was still staring at Earl when her mother nudged her. Earl noticed and immediately sat the pie on the pew behind him, freeing his right hand to aid Lucile and obligating her that much more.

"May we go over to the tables?" Earl coaxed.

Lucile nodded and stood. The couple strolled to the crowded dining area that had been set up in the main hall. Earl found an empty table and assisted Lucile with her chair. He sat down to an awkward silence. Suddenly, he panicked. *Where is the pie?* He had set it on the pew when he gave Lucile his hand. On cue, Arthur sauntered over as if he were a formal waiter and said, in a faux French accent, "your pie, Masseur." He sat the pie on the table and proceeded to just stand there. Earl threw a stabbing glance at Arthur, and in a stressed voice said, "That will be all, Artie."

"Yes, Masseur." Arthur looked at Lucile and dramatically bowed, while saying "Mademoiselle." He then walked away.

Lucile was hiding her smile behind her hand as Earl regained his composure and spoke. "I am so happy to see you here."

Her eyes flashed at him. "You know this is not the pie I brought."

Earl had to think quickly. "Ahh, yes . . . but this is your envelope." He laid it on the table. "Now, I am going to cut you a piece of this fine pie."

Earl served Lucile and then himself before asking, "What brings you and your family to Pleasantville?"

Lucile reluctantly responded, "It is just my mother and I."

There was another pause as each of them took a bite. Feeling awkward, Lucile continued the conversation by asking, "How long have you lived here?"

"All my life . . . well, I mean to say that I have lived in this *area* all my life, just out of town, up on Goodwill Hill."

"I have never heard of Goodwill Hill."

"Let me tell you about it!" Earl exclaimed as the excitement in his voice escalated. "All year round, there is beauty. In winter, the snowflakes dance to the song of the wind as the gusts whisk them across a white canvas like chiffon. In spring, the tapping raindrops arouse the dogwoods to splash white throughout the still barren woods. Flowers then paint the fields as the Mountain Laurel awakens with the trees.

"Summer is made of lush, green meadows and crisp, blue, sunny skies, while the birds sing out in celebration. They fly on lucid air and perch in the trees of shady lanes.

"Come fall, the brightly colored leaves cascade to earth, coloring the ground like a patchwork quilt. They imitate the snowfall of winter, which comes again."

Lucile, dubiously listened to the theatrical description as her mind questioned, *How can someone so backwoods make up such an elaborate explanation?* She replied, "What you describe can be seen in many places."

Earl looked straight into her eyes and said, "Yes."

Unable to respond to what seemed to be a nonsensical reply, Lucile abruptly stood. "Thank you, Mr. Ames. Now, I must find my mother and go. It is getting late, and we have many things to do tomorrow."

Earl nodded as he reluctantly stood and watched her walk away again.

CHAPTER 4
War Declared While Becoming a Tutor

April 7, 1917

Earl stepped onto the old wooden porch. The flexing floorboards gave out their familiar squawks as barking instantly came from inside. He opened the door and stooped as a dog jumped into his arms, almost knocking him down. "Hey, Shep, how are you, old boy?" Earl said as he roughly petted the animal. Shep eagerly licked Earl's face while rapidly wagging his tail. Earl stood and called out, "Father! Mama! You home?"

A comforting voice called out, "We are in the dining room!"

Earl tugged the door shut as he walked in. Shep strutted alongside him. Earl entered the dining room and spied his mother Ella, a tall, thin, gray-haired woman with a strong personality, rummaging through the tableware drawer. "You are just in time," she said while pulling a knife and fork out and setting them on the table.

Little Clara, the youngest sibling, stood at the kitchen door dressed in an apron that was so large that only her shoes peeked out from beneath it. The eight-year-old smiled and gingerly said, "We are having flapjacks, and I made them!"

"My," Earl remarked with a smile, "you are growing up so fast. I am sure your flapjacks will be just as good as Mama's."

"Better," Clara giggled while fidgeting with the wooden spoon in her hand.

"I heard that," Ella joked. "We have to go get them, now."

Ella walked to the kitchen as Clara followed.

Almon, Earl's father, a stout, short man with a reserved disposition, sat at the old round clawfoot table. He glanced up from his newspaper. "Good to see you, Top . . . what brings my eldest son out this way?"

"As long as you have nothing planned, I thought it would be a good day to cut some of that firewood you wanted help with."

"Ahh . . . yes . . ." Almon replied as his eyes flashed back to the paper. "Artie and Albo stayed over at your grandmother's last night. Romey needed them to do some things. If not for that, they could have helped."

"Oh," Earl responded, sensing a touch of anxiety in his father's response.

Earl took a seat at the table across from Almon, which was an unspoken signal for Shep to lie down in the corner. Just then, Clara, with Ella's help, carried a heaping plate of flapjacks into the room. Ella directed Clara as they served Almon and then Earl. Ella set the rest of the cakes in the center of the table while Clara climbed into her chair and served herself. Ella did the same while cautioning, "Remember, Clara, your flapjacks are hot. Blow on every bite before you put it in your mouth."

Clara smiled while shaking her head *yes*.

No one talked as they began to eat, until Ella asked, "Did I tell you that Grandma is thinking of selling her farm and moving to Titusville?"

"No."

"She feels it is just too much for her and your Uncle Romey to handle. I wish your father and I could afford to buy it. That way we could all live there. But, with the amount of money she owes, it is financially out of our reach. We will probably spend the rest of our days living here, renting this old company-owned house."

"What will Uncle Romey do?" Earl asked.

"Mr. Holtz has offered him a job. Part of the wages is that he can live in Holtz's bunkhouse shanty."

"Mama," Almon spoke up. "I smell the flapjacks. Do they need flipping?"

"Oh my, yes! I forgot!" Ella spouted as she immediately stood while wiping her hands on her apron. She grabbed Clara from the chair and said, "Come on, we must check your flapjacks."

"Yes, yes," Clara responded as Ella helped her hastily walk to the stove.

Almon watched them leave before whispering, "Did you see the paper today?"

"No," Earl responded.

Almon waved his hand for Earl to speak quieter. He flipped the front page over and slid the newspaper across the table. The headline jumped off the page: RESOLUTION FOR WAR IS PASSED.

Almon glanced over at the kitchen door to see where Ella and Clara were.

Earl's eyes were still focused on the headline as Almon talked just above a whisper. "I am telling you what I will be telling your brothers. You are *not* to join up. We are patriots, but this family has paid dearly already, with both of your grandfathers fighting in the Civil War . . . it ruined their lives; it affected their families."

"It says here the government is going to raise a million-man army," Earl pointed out. "It also says there will be a conscription."

A sadness crossed Almon's face as he somberly responded, "If you get called . . . then, you will go. Now, take this paper with you. I do not want your mother to know this just yet."

Earl rolled the newspaper and slipped it into his back pocket just before Ella and Clara walked back into the room, "Well," Ella said, "you men better eat up. Here are more—and you have not finished what is on the table." She then sat down another stacked serving plate.

The family talked of other things before Almon and Earl spent the rest of the day cutting, splitting, and stacking firewood.

As Earl walked home that evening, his thoughts drifted to the headline. Questions arose in his mind. *I am not afraid to go to war, but how will I be able to keep my farm? Will I be able to get my lease jobs back afterward? How long might I be gone?*

Upon reaching his farm, he went directly to the barn to feed

Dolly. As the horse nonchalantly munched away, Earl told her all his troubles. Finally he realized that the horse was not concerned. Surrendering to Dolly's indifference, Earl said goodnight and closed the barn door.

He went to the house and stoked the wood stove. The only sound in the room was the crackling of the burning wood as he lit the oil lamp and turned up the wick as far as possible. It shone ever so brightly, warding off the gloom. He pulled the newspaper from his back pocket and dropped it on the floor in front of the old wooden rocker. The rocker was a gift from his grandmother, and had been his grandfather's. It creaked as Earl sat down and leaned back.

That sound always brought back memories of Grandmother telling of how Granddad John would sit on this old rocker on the porch and stare out over the fields. She said there was always a far-off stare in his eyes, brought on by drink and the demons inside him that conjured up horrific memories of the Civil War. Earl leaned forward in the rocker as he wondered, *Did Grandad face these same questions?* Earl thought back to the time when Grandmother said she had asked John about the war. The only response she'd received was, "A man spends a lifetime trying to forget all of that."

Suddenly, a revelation came to Earl. *That is it! Dolly is not concerned and Grandad, in his own way, said to just forget it. The draft has not started, yet! And, for that matter, I may never get conscripted.* A feeling of relief came over Earl. He put everything out of his mind and picked up the paper. Immediately he turned to page seven where the help wanted ads were listed. He instinctively glanced through them like he had many times before, looking for an odd job. Suddenly, his eyes focused on a name in one ad. 'Lake'. He immediately began to read.

WANTED: someone to give my daughter piano lessons, reference required.

Contact E. Lake, 2 East Street, Pleasantville, in person, write, or phone 417

That last name. It must be her! His eyes stared at the advertisement as his mind questioned, *Is this fate, or destiny?*

The next morning Earl awoke early. No work today. The roads had just been dragged, eliminating the deep ruts, and a heavy morning dew would keep the dust down. He could ride his bicycle. He fed Dolly before wheeling the bike from the barn. He jumped on and pedaled to town. The cool morning carried the smell of fragrant fresh air as the far-off call of a chickadee seemed to provide reassurance that he had made the right decision.

Reaching Pleasantville, he clumsily leaned the bike against the alley wall of the livery stable and walked over to the small crowd waiting for the trolley car.

Soon, the noisy contraption rumbled down the tracks in the middle of the street. When it stopped, Earl boarded with the others. He gave the conductor his twelve cents and sat down in the first available seat. As the trolley began to move, the familiar squeaking of the wheels and the vibrations and occasional sway of the moving car alerted all passengers that the trolley was now in control of their destination.

He stared out the window as a gentle breeze lightly tossed his hair. The buildings, and then trees and fields, slowly passed by. The tracks rode smoother at the landing at Fieldmore Springs. The large building that stood on the hill in the background was once a place of great gala, a grand health resort for the wealthy because of the surrounding mineral springs. Now, just an occasional guest would wait on the weathered benches, sitting by the large, unkept urns.

The trolley passed by, then rumbled over the bridge as it traveled on down the hill. Soon it was making its way through the many automobiles, horse-drawn buggies, wagons, and pedestrians on the bustling brick streets of Titusville. Earl stepped off at West Spring Street and walked the crowded sidewalk to Strouse & Benson's. As he entered, an older clerk with a waxed mustache greeted him. "May I help you today, young man?"

"I am here to buy new clothes." Earl timidly said.

"I could not agree more," the clerk responded as he grabbed Earl by the arm and pulled him directly to the suits. The clerk spun around and said, "Now, what occasion will this be for?"

"Ahh?" Earl muttered, unsure of the answer.

"A party?" the clerk guessed.

"No."

"A wedding?"

"Well, no."

"A wake?"

"My, no!"

The clerk stood dumbfounded until Earl finally muttered, "Perhaps it is a recital."

"A recital?" the clerk questioned. "Would this be a formal recital requiring a tuxedo with tails?"

Earl shook his head no.

The confused clerk finally asked, "Would this recital perhaps be to impress a young lady?"

Earl nodded.

"Well, now that we have established the reason, follow me." The clerk stepped down the long line of suits and stopped. "These are some of the most dapper new styles for spring, directly from Europe."

Soon Earl was dressed in a sharp white suit, standing in front of a full-length mirror.

"No altering will be needed. It fits you perfectly," the clerk commented.

"I will buy this one."

"Splendid choice, sir. But the look is not complete." The clerk immediately hurried away, returning with a tie, shirt, and a straw boater hat. "This will leave the young lady with an image of you that she will not forget," the clerk boasted, and hesitated as he looked down at Earl's old muddy shoes and shook his head. "The foot apparel must be replaced."

"What?" Earl responded, not wanting to understand the remark.

Earl purchased the suit with vest for eighteen dollars and fifty cents, a silk crocheted tie for seventy-five cents, a silk shirt for a dollar, new leather shoes for three dollars, and a new boater hat for two dollars. He reluctantly paid as the clerk finished wrapping his purchases in brown paper, tied up with string. "May I make a last suggestion, sir?" the clerk asked without waiting for a response. "To make the finest impression on this young lady, I personally would make a trip to a barbershop and then a bathhouse." Earl stared at the clerk before reluctantly nodding.

Upon leaving the store, Earl made his way directly to a barbershop and then on to the YMCA. People belonged to the YMCA for many reasons. Some country dwellers without indoor plumbing belonged for a place to take what was called "a shower bath."

Earl quickly dressed in his new clothes and wrapped his old clothes in the brown paper that his purchase had been wrapped in. A few women glanced at him as he boarded the 2 pm car back to Pleasantville. He stepped off the trolley on Main Street, grabbed his bicycle, tied his old clothes to the back, and rode directly to East Street. He stopped at her sidewalk and leaned the bike against the white picket fence. He opened the sidewalk gate as doubt crept in.

Will she rebuke me at the door? Is it too late? . . . To come this far, and now turn away, I will wonder forever what could have been. He regained his courage and walked the long sidewalk. He stepped up onto the porch and knocked on the door as his heart raced. He heard footsteps coming, and could see a silhouette through the lace curtains that hung in the door's window. The curtains flicked, the door opened . . . and there she stood.

"Yes?" Lucile asked the dashing young man. Earl froze as Lucile stared directly into his deep blue eyes, recognizing him.

"I am here…" Earl blurted out as he thought, *I am making a fool of myself.* "I mean, I am here to give lessons." *Did that sound right?*

She giggled. "I do not want trombone lessons."

"No," Earl spoke up. "Piano lessons."

Just then Lucile's mother called out from the adjoining parlor, "Lucile, who is at the door?"

"It is the trombone player, mother . . . the one from the pie social. He is here from the advertisement."

"Tell him it is piano lessons we require, not trombone."

Earl had to think fast. He spied a grand piano sitting to the right of the room by a large window.

"The advertisement says a reference is required . . . may I?" He pointed to the piano.

Lucile raised her brow and hesitated. Finally, she opened the door just far enough for Earl to squeeze by. He nervously fumbled with his hat before pushing it into Lucile's hands.

Earl immediately walked to the beautiful instrument, admiring it with every step he took. He sat down and gently lifted the fallboard, revealing shimmering white ivory. His fingers glided across the keys, not making a sound as they barely touched them. He stared at the glittering keys one last time before he put his hands toward the center and pushed down on one key. The clarity of that pure note echoed endlessly. He began to play. The music flowed incessantly from the instrument, coaxing Lucile's mother from the adjoining room. Both women listened intently as Earl put unbridled emotion into every note.

The serenade finally closed as the last note echoed endlessly. Earl sat silently, taking one last look at the keys. He gently pulled down the fallboard and remarked, "The grandest instrument I have ever played." He looked up at Lucile and Eleanor, who were staring back in awe.

"How beautiful," Lucile remarked.

"Yes," her mother agreed as she took her handkerchief and dabbed her eyes.

"What work is it?" Lucile asked.

"Claude Debussy," Earl replied. "The Girl with the Flaxen Hair."

Lucile instinctively touched her hair, a reaction that told Earl he had picked the perfect song.

"Where did you ever learn to play so elegantly?" Eleanor asked.

"My mama . . . from the time we were small, she insisted that all her children learn to play an instrument. She chose me, her firstborn, to play her favorite instrument, the piano. Mama loves the classics. I have played them for her time and time again, but I prefer more current composers like Debussy."

"You play the piano so beautifully, why the trombone?" Lucile inquisitively asked.

"The marching band," was all Earl had to say.

He stayed for dinner and got the tutoring job.

CHAPTER 5

Bull Chase, Drilling, and Fishing

Mid-April 1917

Sunbeams broke through the trees at the field's edge, throwing stripes of light across the ground. That daybreak found Earl already guiding a team of horses plowing. He pulled back on the reins. "Whoa." Dolly and Prince seemed to agree, they instantly halted and began flipping their tails. Earl took a deep breath of fresh morning air before shrugging the canteen strap from his shoulder. He twisted off the cap and took a long drink. Dolly snorted and scuffed the dirt with her hoof.

"All right, all right, I know both of you are thirsty, too. We will stop at the creek on our next pass." Earl popped the lid back on the canteen and shouldered it to his side just as someone hollered out his nickname. "Top!"

Earl looked around to see a stout young man with dark wavy hair trotting toward him. It was his brother Albert.

"Hello, Albo," Earl said when Albert reached him. "What brings you out here this forenoon?"

"The neighbor, Everly Dane."

A puzzled look crossed Earl's face before Albert explained, "He asked me to feed his livestock because he had to go to town early today, but that bull of his was not in the barn where he was supposed to be, so I walked out into the pasture, looking for him. Next thing I know, the animal is chasing me. I swear that I ran faster than my legs could carry me and ended up jumping the fence to escape." Albert pointed to the bull, still standing at the fence and staring his way. "Then I look up, and there you are . . . so I decided to come visit."

Earl snickered and responded, "You seem calm, after all of that. I know that bull is a vile one. How fast did you say he made you run, again?"

"It is not funny," Albert huffed. "I do not know why Everly keeps such an angry animal around."

"Because he thinks that bull can take first prize at the Titusville Fair," Earl replied.

Albert got defensive. "Well, if it was my bull, prize or not, Mama would be cooking steak tonight."

Albert changed the subject. "Did you read the paper yesterday?"

"No, been busy."

"Well, President Wilson has signed a selective draft act. I guess that makes it final. We are going to war."

Albert waited for Earl's reaction, but received none. Albert continued, "I hope to get conscripted . . . but they are only taking ages twenty-one to thirty, now." Immediately, Albert changed the topic. "You should buy one of those steam-powered traction engines. That way, you would not need to borrow Prince from Father."

Earl chuckled. "For all our two little farms produce, none of us could afford that. Now, I must get to work, or we will never finish today. I also promised these two that they get to drink from the creek on our next pass . . . and you have an angry bull to feed."

"You are too humorous, brother," Albert responded, before adding, "by the way, Artie is over on the Weldon lease, cutting off a new well location. Holtz is expecting you to be there when he brings in that Wolfe rig of his."

"I know," Earl piped up. "But I have so much on my plate. He pays good. Maybe you could do that job?"

"No," Albert abruptly replied. "He wants you. Besides, I am a tool dresser first, a pumper second. Rig hand is way down the list, for me."

"Father taught you well," Earl responded.

Albert ignored the remark and continued, "Artie said for you to cut an extra cord of wood because there will not be enough coming off the location."

"You are full of wonderful news today," Earl responded sarcastically.

"Yes," Albert replied before he asked Earl, "What time are we going to meet at the Patriotic Rally on the 20th?"

"I did not know anything about it. Besides, that is more than a week from now."

Albert shook his head. "Well, you should know anyway. The band is marching in it. We are to meet at the open lot just down from town square. From what I hear, there is going to be a lot of people and veterans, and some general is coming to speak."

Albert added, "By the way, the water tank wagon needs to be filled. It is over at Herb's lease."

"Are you going back over the fence?" Earl interjected before another task escaped Albert's mouth.

"No . . . I think that I will walk around," Albert replied apprehensively.

Earl smiled at Albert and then flipped the reins. The plow jerked as the team began to pull again. Albert watched until Earl and the horses disappeared over the brow of the open field. He then turned and walked back to Dane's barn.

Earl and the team worked until late afternoon. "Whoa," Earl finally said. "It is time to quit. We must get home so that I have time to clean up before going to give piano lessons to the prettiest girl I have ever seen."

Prince stood still as Dolly acted almost insulted. She shook her head and her mane gracefully swayed as she neighed.

"I know . . . I know, you are also pretty," Earl consoled as he patted Dolly on the side. He unhooked the team from the plow, grabbed the reins, and led them to the barn.

Earl cleaned up, put on his new clothes, and strapped a satchel over his shoulder that contained his music pages. He grabbed his bicycle from the barn and rode to town. Soon he was knocking at her door. It swung open. There stood Lucile, staring at him as her mind remarked, *Is this the only suit of clothes this man owns?* She came to her senses, saying, "Hello, Mr. Ames. You are right on time. Please come in."

Earl smiled as he stepped inside. He took off his hat and hung it on the hall coatrack, then stood until Lucile lifted her hand toward the piano and said, "Shall we?"

"Yes," Earl replied.

They sat down on the piano bench and then, side by side, Earl began to teach her the same way his mother had taught him. Lucile seemed to learn the keys very quickly as the hour flew by. During that time, their apprehension subsided, and the two talked and giggled. Earl finished the session with a piano serenade before they walked toward the door. He retrieved his hat as an awkward pause arose. Finally, he blurted out, "Would you care to go fishing?"

"Fishing!" Lucile said loudly, in surprise.

Before she could answer, Earl rushed out the door. With his back turned toward her, he mumbled, "I will pick you up Saturday forenoon." Lucile could not understand his incoherent words.

Earl returned home, put on his old clothes and went back to work. He hitched up Dolly and Prince and led them to Herb's farm where they picked up the water wagon and filled it at a nearby pond. Earl then directed the horses to pull the heavy wagon across the field that lay before the well location. The wagon's wheels cut into the soil more than Earl felt they should.

After leaving the water wagon at the location, Earl led the horses back to the barn before cutting and loading firewood by lantern light. It was very late when he finished. Exhausted, he sat down in the old rocker and fell asleep.

A drizzle started in the early morning hours, then came to an end by daybreak. But the lingering, gray sky was a warning. Earl hooked Dolly and Prince to the buckboard full of firewood and loaded some wooden planks on top before meeting Arthur at the field.

Earl drove the wagon while Arthur stood in the back and tossed the planks across the soft field soil. When the task was finished, they unloaded the firewood before arranging the scattered planks into a makeshift road. A breeze whispered through a grove of pines that stood nearby as Arthur looked to the sky in a concerned manner, and said, "I hope the rain holds off."

Just then, Earl caught a faint chugging sound and said, "He is coming."

The chugging, along with rattle and swoosh sounds, became louder as the lumbering steam traction engine, with a drilling rig in tow, came into view. Holtz gave a big wave as he reached the two brothers. He then carefully turned the machine onto the makeshift road. The process of planking machinery across a soft field began. The sweat poured down Earl and Arthur's faces as they hastily grabbed planks and aligned them in front of the slow-moving equipment's wheels. Their toil was driven by the fact that if the wheels came off the planks, everything would sink into the mud. It might take hours, if not days, to dig the equipment out again.

One drop, then another—it began to sprinkle, and then the downpour came. The field became a sea of sticky brown as the brothers' boots became blocks of clinging mud, weighing down every step they took. Their clothes were drenched as they labored on, laying the wooden trail. Earl finally took off his hat and tilted his head to the sky. He closed his eyes as the raindrops pelted his face and pondered, *Maybe the raindrops are beautiful, but to work in it is not so.* Suddenly, the rain stopped. Earl opened his eyes in amazement.

He pulled off his glove and pushed back his drenched hair before putting his hat on again. The reprieve might not last long, but they were almost to the clear-cut area. The ground was firmer there.

By late afternoon the crew had the rig on location and blocked, the traction power positioned behind and the flat belt connected. The mast was unfolded and raised, the guy wires anchored and taut. Drilling will start tomorrow. Earl's part of this operation was done. Now his tool dresser brother, Albert, would start his part of the job.

Morning came. Earl finished his chores early, he had Dolly hooked to the wagon and his best work clothes on, and had two fishing rods and a bucket of worms loaded by 5 AM. He began to reason that it might be a bit too early to go to her door, so he waited until 6:00. The predawn glow would light the sky by the time he reached her house.

"Come on, Dolly, let us go," he said while anxiously flipping the reins, starting the horse towards town. Soon he was at Lucile's house. He walked the now-familiar sidewalk and knocked. Lucile groggily opened the door with a puzzled look on her face, "Mr. Ames, it is very early, and my lesson is not until Thursday."

"I am not here for the lesson. We are going fishing."

Lucile's mind flashed back to when Earl had last departed her home. He had said something about going fishing. "I did not understand," she quickly said.

Earl glanced at her with a puzzled look.

"I must change clothes," she immediately added, then slammed the door in his face. Realizing what she had done, she quickly pulled the door back open.

"All right," Earl responded.

"All right, what?" Lucile replied.

"All right, change your clothes. I will wait by the wagon."

"All right," she said. The door clanked shut hard. She had slammed it in his face again. She immediately yanked it back open.

Earl smiled. Lucile smiled back, then softly closed the door. She ran to change as her mind screamed, *Why is he here? Who would ask someone out the first time to go fishing? I do not know how to fish!*

Earl walked back to the wagon, pulled a carrot from his pocket, and fed it to Dolly as they waited.

Finally Lucile stepped out the door, all dressed up in heeled shoes with a matching hat and shawl. She looked as if she was going to church.

Earl stared strangely at her as his mind questioned, *Is she going fishing dressed like that?*

As Lucile reached the sidewalk gate, she said nonchalantly,

"Mother felt we should have a chaperone, but I assured her that you are a gentleman. Besides, what derelict would come to my door this early and want to take me fishing?" Lucile climbed up onto the wagon seat and slid over. She muttered, "You should have brought an automobile."

Earl, stymied by her statement, said nothing as he hopped up onto the wagon seat beside her. He grabbed the reins and flicked them. "Let us go, Dolly." The wagon jerked and off they went.

Earl guided the rig through the morning streets of Pleasantville as an occasional horse, a frequent automobile, and a few lorries passed by. When the trolley approached, Dolly jittered some and stepped sideways.

"It is okay, girl," Earl called out as he pulled back slightly on the reins. Dolly calmed as Earl turned the horse onto a different street.

Soon the couple were out on a country road. As they rode along, the clip-clop of Dolly's hooves and the hollow sound of the rolling wagon wheels on the dirt road were the only sounds. Earl glanced over to Lucile. Her shawl caught his attention as a slight breeze intermittently caressed it. His thoughts dwelled on the revelation that this was the first time he was alone with her. Sensing that he was staring, she turned to him, asking, "Where are we going?"

"Pine Creek, down off the Bug Town Road."

"Bug Town Road!" she repeated aloud as her mind debated, *Who takes a date to some place called 'Bug Town Road'?*

"Yes," Earl responded. "The fishing is good there."

The couple rode on in silence until Earl pulled Dolly off to an open area alongside an old bridge. "Whoa, girl," he calmly commanded, and Dolly brought the wagon to a stop. Earl jumped down and tied the horse to the low-hanging branch of a small tree. He retrieved a bucket of water from the back of the wagon for the horse before sneaking another carrot from his pocket for her. He turned and reached up to help Lucile down. Afterward, he grabbed another bucket and two old bamboo rods from the back of the wagon. He took Lucile's hand and carefully led her through the weeds and brush, along a makeshift path. As the creek came into view, the morning sun was shimmering off the babbling water. Suddenly Earl said, "Stop!"

"What? What?" Lucile worriedly spouted.

"Listen."

"I do not hear anything."

"Yes, you do."

Lucile noticed the far-off, two-tone call of a chickadee. "Yes, I hear it now."

In a meek voice, Earl said, "He is calling out, telling us that no matter what, we are not alone."

"How beautiful. I shall always remember that," Lucile remarked.

The couple listened for a moment longer before moving on. They walked along the bank until they reached a peaceful pool. Earl set down the bucket before handing Lucile a pole. "The worms are in there," he said as he pointed to the bucket.

"What do I do with a worm?"

Between that response and Lucile's attire, it was now obvious to Earl that she had never been fishing. "I will show you," he said as he pulled a worm from the bucket.

Lucile, sickened by the sight, almost gagged as Earl pushed the worm onto the hook. He said, "We are on this side of the creek, so the fish will not see our shadows. Now we must quietly step to the edge, so they do not sense any vibrations and swim away."

Earl stationed Lucile where the water was calm, and the bank was a few feet higher than the creek. He took her rod and gently tossed the baited line into the water. "If you feel some small tugs on your line, give a slight jerk to hook the fish." He handed her the rod and pointed down the creek bank. "I will be just over there if you need help." He then walked away.

Lucile stood, staring intensely at the line in the water until the tranquility of the sun's rays, the occasional rustling sound of a gentle breeze through the trees, and the trickling song of the creek overtook her senses. She closed her eyes. Suddenly she felt a slight tug on her line, then another. On the third tug, she gave the pole a swift yank—

too hard. The line flung into the air above her head as something held onto the end of the hook. The line fell to the ground as a small creature landed beside her shoe. "EEK!" she shrieked as she lurched away and lost her footing. She tumbled into the creek and immediately began struggling to get to her feet. Suddenly, an arm grabbed around her waist and hoisted her up from the shallow water. Coughing and choking, she finally regained her composure enough to push her hair back from her eyes, only to see Earl holding her tightly as they both stood in the water.

"Are you all right?"

"Yes," Lucile replied as she pulled away. "What was that vicious creature on my line?"

Earl smirked, "A crayfish."

Lucile splashed water into Earl's face in anger as she stated, "Whatever it was, I do not see the humor in this!" She noticed Earl prying his eyes away from her and timidly turning around. Lucile looked down to see that her wet cotton dress was clinging tightly to her figure, and had become transparent in some places.

After Earl had turned away, he spied Lucile's shawl floating in the water as his thoughts screamed, *She is beautiful.* He grabbed the garment and wrung it out the best he could before handing it to her from behind his back.

Lucile covered herself with the shawl while Earl rescued her hat. "Hold onto my waist," he commanded as he held onto the hat and led Lucile through the slippery mud and back up onto the bank.

The two stood, wondering what to do next, when Earl finally said, "I will get our gear." He rushed off to pick up everything.

When he came back to Lucile, he offered his free hand and led her back along the narrow path. Dolly stared, as if confused, at the sight of two drenched humans coming toward the wagon. She whinnied, as if chuckling, when they walked by. Earl threw the poles and bucket in the wagon before helping Lucile up onto the seat.

Earl jumped up, fidgeting momentarily before handing Lucile her hat. She quickly grabbed it. Earl flipped the reins while commanding, "Let us go, Dolly." The horse pulled the wagon around and started back towards town.

Silence overshadowed the moment as Lucile shivered while holding her shawl tightly around her body. The everlasting ride finally ended when Earl brought the wagon to a halt at her gate. Lucile immediately jumped off and started up the sidewalk.

Earl called out, "Should I still come by Thursday for your piano lesson?"

Lucile never looked back as she stepped up onto the porch and shouted, "No! Come the following Thursday!" She yanked open the door before slamming it behind her.

CHAPTER 6

The Skunk and the War Rally

April 20, 1917

"Top!" a voice cracked from behind him.

Earl whirled in surprise to see Arthur standing there with a fiendish grin on his face. Arthur asked, "What are you doing?"

Earl regained his composure before wiping the sweat from his brow. "I am trying to dig a skunk out. He has made a home in this hole. Every night, when he comes out, his stench wakes me. I know he has a right to be here too—but not this close to me."

"Well, let me at it for a bit," Arthur commanded as he grabbed the shovel from Earl's hand and pushed him aside.

Earl grabbed his gun, which was leaning against the nearby wood pile. He moved it farther away as Arthur wildly dug.

"So, what brings you out here this afternoon?" Earl inquired.

Arthur never looked up as he answered, "Just thought I would come early to see you before we go to play at that patriotic war rally tonight. I brought my horn and uniform with me so that we can leave from here."

The scraping sound of the shovel sliding past a rock interrupted Arthur. He stopped digging momentarily and turned to Earl. "You did not forget again, did you?"

"No," Earl replied with a contrived confidence on his face, before asking, "will Father and Mama be going?"

"I doubt it, You know how Mama feels about war . . . the band is meeting on South Main Street. We then march toward the town square behind the Boy Scouts, to the Methodist Church."

Arthur went back to digging as he remarked, "We were going to play inside during the rally, but the I.O.O.F formed a band just recently, and they are playing that part."

Arthur bent down to lift the rock that he had just dug out from the side of the hole when he abruptly stopped and loudly whispered, "Look! Fur!"

Earl grabbed his gun just as the creature scampered backward with its tail lifted.

"Shoot! Shoot!" Arthur frantically shouted as he threw the rock while jumping from the hole. BANG!

"Confound it!"

The two spent the rest of the afternoon disposing of the skunk, filling in the hole, and retrieving Earl's galvanized tub from the barn and filling it with hot water heated on the stove. Mama's lye soap took off the dirt, but not the smell. Soon they were taking turns bathing in jar tomato juice from Earl's root cellar. Both brothers changed into their band uniforms and threw their tainted garments into the tub of juice. "I will hang them on the clothesline tomorrow and let them air for a few weeks. Between the rain and the sun, the smell will go away," Earl said reassuringly.

"Do I still smell like skunk?" Arthur asked.

"Here, put some of this on." Earl handed Arthur a bottle of cologne, never answering Arthur's question.

Arthur splashed a little on before Earl leaned toward him to smell. "Put more on."

Afterward, Earl also splashed on a large amount of cologne.

The two hooked Dolly to the wagon and headed for town. Upon arriving, they tied the horse to a hitching post located far up the street, because the sidewalks were filled with a giant crowd. "There must be six hundred people here," Arthur remarked as the two pulled their instruments from their cases and started walking to the other side of town. Suddenly, someone from the crowd called out, "Top! Artie! Wait up." It was Albert, pushing his way toward them. When he reached Earl and Arthur, he remarked, "Where have you two been? It is getting late."

The two said nothing until Albert crinkled his nose and leaned toward Arthur, and then toward Earl. He recognized an odor that was separate from the cologne.

"You two smell a bit overripe," Albert remarked.

"Albo, you can smell it?" Earl questioned in amazement.

Albert rolled his eyes. "Yes, I can smell it, or I would not have said anything."

"We got that skunk," Arthur injected confidently.

"Well, I am glad you told me that, Artie," Albert remarked, "or I would have thought the skunk had won."

"Let us go, or we will be late," Earl remarked, bringing a halt to the sarcasm.

Just then, Jack Litzinger, wearing his uniform and with trumpet in hand, walked up to the three brothers, "Greetings, men. Where is the band meeting?" Jack was immediately acknowledged with two scowling stares and one indifferent look.

"On the other side of town," Albert answered. "Follow us."

Jack fell in behind the brothers and immediately stated, "I smell skunk."

"No," Earl abruptly replied, "you smell Artie's cologne."

"Really?" Jack replied in amazement, before mumbling, "Well Artie, if you think it is going to get you a girl . . . you are very wrong."

Nothing more was said as the crowd seemed to miraculously give way for the boys to pass.

They reached the rendezvous point and took their places in the band formation. The local Boy Scouts, dressed in full uniform, fell in just ahead of the band. A drummer and color guard positioned themselves at the front. A big black Packard automobile pulled up behind them just as the color guard began to march in place. The drumbeat started, the procession began moving, the band leader raised his baton, and the band began to play "America." The crowd chimed in, singing, as the parade moved. Loud applause and cheering, mixed with singing and music, filled the air as the parade made its way through the village.

Reaching the church, the color guard marched up the steps as the band aligned on one side of the sidewalk and the Scouts aligned on the other side. The Packard stopped at the sidewalk and the dignitaries exited. All were dressed in military uniforms—obviously they were veterans of the Civil and Spanish-American Wars. The old soldiers waved to the cheering people as they walked into the church.

Instantly, Jack jumped in behind the dignitary group as if he was supposed to be there. He disappeared into the crowd that filled the sidewalk and church to overcapacity.

Unable to get in, Earl, Albert, and Arthur stood outside with many other people. After a time, they heard loud applause coming from inside. A bold male voice began a stirring speech.

Suddenly, Albert blurted out, "The back door!" Immediately the three brothers took off, still carrying their instruments. Reaching the door, they quietly opened it and walked in behind the people standing on stage. No one seemed to notice as they squeezed in among the color guard to the right of the assembly . . . no one except the drummer, who pinched his nose and moved over.

Major General W. J. Hulings was giving a stirring speech. "Liberty is one of our greatest gifts!" he charged, "but there is a price to be paid for liberty!" The general continued fervently talking as sporadic, rousing applause came from the crowd. (This event was published in the Titusville Hearld Newspaper the next day, April 21, 1917, on Page 2.)

Afterward, the American flag was carried to the center of the stage and the Pledge of Allegiance was recited before the Star-Spangled Banner was sung, accompanied by the I.O.O.F band. The rally ended with a dramatic fireworks display outside. The brothers watched the fiery explosions until Earl glanced across the crowd. He spied a girl who was turned away from him. She was intently gazing up at the many bursts and flashes. His brothers never noticed as Earl nudged his way through an ocean of people until he was standing directly behind her. He reached out and gently touched her shoulder . . . and she turned. Earl's eyes opened wide, "Oh, pardon me. I thought you were someone else."

CHAPTER 7
The United States Boys Working Reserve

Early May 1917

I t had been two weeks. It was now the second Thursday. *Tonight, I see her,* Earl thought as he went about his work.

It was time to run the oil. Upon reaching the first well, he took his mallet in hand and gave a swift whack to the large wooden plug on the side of the separating tank. He wiggled it free and barely pulled it out, allowing the saltwater to spray from around the plug until the stream turned to greenish crude. He immediately shoved the plug back in and whacked it tight. He grabbed the makeshift wrench leaning against a nearby tree and inserted it onto the gate-valve at the bottom of the tank. He turned the valve until it was straight. The oil began to flow down the long pipeline to the large collection tank at the bottom of the hill. After the crude had emptied, he closed everything up and moved on to do the same to the next well.

Tomorrow, the gauger would come to measure the amount in the collection tank. Afterwards, the oil would be picked up, the lease owner would be paid by the refinery, and then it would be Earl's turn to get a paycheck.

As the sunlight twinkled through the trees, his mind reverted to Lucile again as questions arose. *What shall I say when she comes to her door? Will I be greeted kindly? Or coldly?* But only that moment would give the answers. He blocked those thoughts from his mind and continued working until the day was done.

By afternoon, he was standing at her door once more. His shaking hand drew back from knocking before he took control and followed through. He heard someone on the other side. The door swung open . . . and there she stood.

"Come in," Lucile said with an unreadable look on her face. She opened the door wider for Earl to pass. He stepped in and hung his hat on the hat tree before turning to her. "Shall we get started?"

"Yes," Lucile replied as she made her way to the piano. Earl followed.

The two sat down before Earl conjured up his best authoritative teacher voice and said, "Let us begin by playing the scales."

"No," Lucile replied.

"No?" Earl asked in a dumbfounded tone. Lucile looked into his eyes and said, "I want you to listen." She lifted the fallboard, put her fingers on the keys, took a deep breath, and began to play. Through the erratic tempo and occasional spasmodic stop, Earl easily recognized the Debussy piece, "The Girl with the Flaxen Hair." Lucile forged on until the last note of the piece faded away. She looked at Earl, waiting for a response.

"You have been practicing," Earl said, missing the obscure meaning.

"Yes."

Earl timidly spoke. "I am sorry . . ."

Lucile quickly touched her finger to his lips, stopping a needless apology.

"Shall we continue?" she asked as she began to play the scales.

Earl put his hand down on hers, interrupting the practice. The notes echoed away as he said, "Let us start over."

"What do you mean?"

Earl solemnly spoke. "My name is Earl . . . the magic that surrounds you has led me here . . . to glimpse the hope . . . for a peerless destiny."

Lucile's eyes opened wide as Earl leaned ever closer to her. She glanced away and regained her composure before stuttering, "Well, Mr. Ames, let us be done for today. We will continue next Thursday." She immediately stood.

Noting that his forwardness had been rejected and that the time spent was very short, Earl slowly rose from the bench, walked over to the hall tree, retrieved his hat, then let himself out the door. He left without taking his money for the lesson, which always lay on top of the small table by the door.

The next day found Earl working on the Weldon lease. A tree had fallen on the jerk line and crushed the tripod that led to well number twelve. Earl was swinging his axe, chopping the limbs away, when he caught site of a woman in the distance. She was walking along the jerk line, towards him. He stopped as she approached.

"Hello, Earl."

"Hello, Miss Chelmadine," Earl replied with a puzzled expression on his face.

She smiled and said, "I asked Arthur where I might find you, and he told me you would be here." She glanced around before closing her eyes and taking a deep breath. "I had forgotten how beautiful this place is." She further delayed the reason for her presence by revealing something personal. "I must tell you that when I was a little girl, my grandparents lived here on Goodwill Hill. I remember everything just as it was . . . as if it were yesterday." She silently reminisced a moment longer, then looked directly at Earl and stated, "But what brings me here today, is you."

"Me?"

"Yes . . .you have not been in class for a while."

"I know. I joined that new program, 'The United States Boys Working Reserve'. They gave me a card that allows me to leave school. I added working on Everly Dane's farm to qualify; plus I still run my farm and work three oil leases."

Miss Chelmadine instantly replied, "I know you do, Earl, and it is very patriotic of you to help. With so many men going off to war, our nation has no choice but to use such a program to fill the vacancies in the labor force. If our farms are not able to bring their crops to harvest, we could face tragedy." She hesitated before saying, "I probably should not tell you this . . . but many times I have marveled at the work you hand in . . . your ability to play any instrument you take interest in . . . your detail in the bird and insect dissection drawings I had the class do . . . you are the most brilliant student I have ever had the privilege to teach. Because of that, you must look to your own future. You have the ability to be something more."

"Look around," Earl stoutly replied. "My future is surrounding us right now. Just like my father's, and my grandfather's, and his father before him . . . and now that the war is here, you know the conscription is coming."

"Earl, that may mean nothing. None of us know what tomorrow might bring. This does not have to be the end of your future unless you want it to be."

Earl flashed his eyes away while rudely turning back to his work. Miss Chelmadine stood in stunned silence before making her final remark. "If you do not come back to school in the fall, you are still eligible to take the test to graduate . . . please do so." She then turned away. Earl looked back after she had left. He watched her walk along the jerk line until she disappeared down the ridge. His mind, all the while, dwelled on her words. (Earl would do what Miss Chelmadine asked and took the graduation test in the fall. He passed with flying colors.)

After his encounter with Miss Chelmadine, Earl finished his work and ventured over to Pineville to see his parents. When he reached the house and knocked, Albert and Shep met him at the door. "Hey, Top, what brings you here this evening?"

"Just wanted to say hello," Earl responded as he stooped to pat the dog's head.

"I just got home myself," Albert replied.

"Are Mama and Father here?" Earl asked as he looked up at Albert.

"I saw them along with Russell and Clara out back, working in the garden."

"All right." Earl said as he gave Shep one last pat, and then stood to leave.

"Wait!" Albert spouted as he glanced around to make sure

everyone was still out of hearing distance. He quietly spoke. "I am glad you came over. It will save me a trip to your house. Will you come watch me fight on Thursday night?"

"You are not going to fight Jack Litzinger again, are you?"

"Of course not. He is my best friend, now. But Jack lined me up for a bare knuckle fight up in Tidioute, against some rig hand from that Universal Drilling Company."

"Albo, that is a good-size operation, not some little locally owned lease. They may have a real ringer to fight you."

"Come on, Top," Albert pleaded. "Artie is coming, and I want you to be there too . . . Besides, I get five dollars whether I win or not. I will be able to pay you for those traps."

Earl's mind raced. *Thursday is Lucile's piano lesson. There will be no way to be there and make the fight also. It probably would not matter to her anyway.*

"All right," Earl finally agreed.

"Great!" Albert quickly injected. "I want you to bring Dolly and your wagon, also."

"Why?"

"Well . . . you just never know what it might be needed for." Albert gave his usual fiendish grin and slapped Earl on the back. "Now, go see Mama and Father. I got some preparing to do."

Earl shook his head as he turned from Albert and walked around back. Shep followed along.

"Hello," Earl called out.

"Well, hello, Top," Almon replied as he looked up from hoeing. Ella stood from kneeling, stepped over to Earl, and gave him a big hug. Clara ran over and did the same. Russell gave a wave from a distance.

"This is a pleasant surprise," Ella remarked.

"I was not far away, and thought I would come visit."

"Well, I am so glad you did. Are you feeling all right? You look thin."

"Yes, Mama, I am fine."

"Well, visit with your father for a bit while I go in and heat something up to eat. Then we can visit some more." Ella then said, "Come on, Clara, we have a meal to prepare."

Clara followed her mother into the house as Almon resumed hoeing, not looking up as he asked, "How have you been, son?"

"I have been alright. Been busy pumping leases, getting the fields ready for planting, and giving music lessons. How about you?"

"Just been doing the same things—pumping and maintaining the Carlen lease. It has been twenty-five years, now." Almon quit hoeing and glanced over to see where Russell was. He then looked at Earl. "I have been bothered, lately, though. There is a rumor going around that Carlen is going to sell out to some big company named Universal Drilling."

"Really?"

"Yes, and if that happens and they do not take me on . . . well, I do not know what Mama and I would do."

"Surely, they will keep you," Earl confidently replied. "You know more about Carlen's fifty wells and his three power houses than anyone."

Almon stood silent and then said, "Top, things are going to change. Nothing stays the same forever." Almon went back to hoeing just as Ella called out from the back door, "All three of you, come get something to eat before Albert empties every dish."

CHAPTER 8
Bare Knuckles Fighting

Mid-May 1917

"Whoa, girl," Earl commanded as he pulled back on the reins. He jumped from the wagon seat and lashed Dolly to a rail, then grabbed the water bucket from the back of the wagon and set it beside her. Dolly looked at him, expecting something more. Earl noticed and grabbed the carrot he always carried in his pocket. "Here you go, girl."

Earl looked around at the many buildings. Muffled sounds were coming from a barn across the way. He walked to the door and knocked. It swung open as a stranger stood looking at him.

"The bets go to me," the man commanded as he reached out his hand. Earl was stymied for a moment, then reached in his pocket and pulled out a quarter. The stranger glanced at the piddly bet before asking, "Who are you putting this on?"

"Albo."

"Albo?" The man questioned. "You mean 'The Kid'?"

Earl hesitated again, and blurted out, "Yes!"

The man wrote 'twenty-five cents, Kid' on a slip of paper and handed it to Earl before letting him pass on into the dingily lit building.

Earl glanced around. The equipment and tools had all been piled up along the outside walls, allowing space for a large group of shabby-looking men to gather in the center. Earl slowly nudged through the crowd until he spied Albert, Arthur, and Jack all standing together to the left.

When Earl reached the three, he grinned and exclaimed, "The Kid?"

"Jack told them that," Albert complained while flashing a grimace towards Jack.

"I thought it sounded tougher than 'Albo'," Jack nonchalantly replied.

"Well, you are going to need any help you can get," Arthur piped up as he pointed to a giant of a man pulling his shirt off. He was obviously Albert's opponent.

"Look at the height of that man," Arthur remarked out loud.

"Good," Albert responded.

"What do you mean, 'good'?" Arthur asked, astonished.

"He has farther to fall than me."

Just then, a man called out, "Alright, everyone make room."

The crowd immediately created a circular opening in the middle of the barn floor.

Albert pulled off his shirt and started bouncing around to warm up. The referee stepped into the circle and waved for the two fighters to come to the middle. Albert enthusiastically ran out as his opponent confidently walked out. Cheers and jeers came from the crowd as Arthur screamed out over the noise, "The Kid!" He turned and muttered to Earl, "I cannot bear to watch. This will be like the Easter Bunny fighting Goliath."

The crowd noise escalated further as the officiator stepped back from the two contenders and the joust began. Albert bounced about his opponent like a puppy hopping around an older dog. One . . . two . . . Albert landed a few small punches before ducking a powerful swooping swing from his adversary. The two sparred on as the crowd anxiously yelled for more contact. Suddenly the big man threw a hard right and connected. Like a kite snatched by the wind, Albert flew backwards into the crowd. A couple of patrons grabbed his arms and immediately tossed him back into the circle. Stunned, Albert shook his head to regain his composure just as the big man stepped forward and gave him another blow. Once more, Albert flew into the crowd; and once more the crowd tossed him back. Albert stood back and shook his head again while spitting blood. His breathing was hard, his eye was swelling shut. His mind finally focused when he heard Jack's voice yelling over the crowd, "Protect yourself!"

Jack then turned to Arthur and Earl and griped, "I could do better! That guy is lucky *I* am not out there!"

Both brothers stared at Jack as Arthur said, "If you think that, why did you get this fight for Albo?"

Jack ignored the question, acting as if he had not heard it over the crowd's noise.

Albert took Jack's suggestion and pulled back from a few swings as his mind began shouting, *This is only dragging things out!* Suddenly Albert screamed, "I have had enough!" Determination and adrenalin overtook his soul. He clinched his fists tighter and darted in close, ducking the blows with lightning moves. His challenger missed once . . . twice . . . three times.

Earl and Arthur noticed the same weakness at the same moment as Albert had—the big man was not protecting his ribs. "Put the bug on him!" both brothers screamed in unison.

Albert's mind flashed, *Got to time this perfectly!* He pranced around for a moment before jumping toward his opponent and dropping lightning fast into a stoop. A power swing passed over his head as Albert sprung up and forward, punching the big man's unprotected ribs. In a split second, Albert was behind his opponent. The man spun around, unprepared, and met Albert's knuckles. Stunned, the man dropped his arms. That was Albert's chance. He began rabbit punching his opponent's face over and over, like rapidly firing a gun. Both men tumbled to the floor with Albert on top, still attacking. Every person in the barn was shouting. Suddenly, Albert recognized someone's voice screaming, "Albo! Stop! Albo! Stop!"

Albert was pulled off his adversary. Blood dripped from Albert's mouth and nose. His eye was swollen shut, and his breathing was heavy and intense. His body was covered in sweat. The exhaustion barely allowed him to raise his fist and shout, "I told you he had farther to fall!"

The excitement was over as fast as it had started. The crowd dissipated as Arthur and Earl helped Albert to Earl's wagon. Earl dipped a rag into Dolly's water bucket and wiped Albert's face. "Here, hold this on your eye," Earl said.

"How do I look?" Albert asked.

"Terrible," Earl replied.

"You look better than the other guy," Arthur consoled.

Arthur and Earl squeezed Albert in between them on the wagon seat, to keep him propped up. Just then Jack walked over. "Here is your prize money, Albo."

Albert reached out as Jack stuffed a few bills into his hand.

"Top, you need to go back in and collect your winnings," Jack suggested.

"No, Albo needs to go home," Earl reached into his pocket and pulled out the bid slip. "Here, it is yours."

"Thanks!" Jack said as he spun around and headed back for the barn.

"Let us go, Dolly," Earl said as he flipped the reins.

The three brothers sat quietly as the horse pulled the wagon through the darkness. Albert would occasionally fidget, trying to ward off the pain.

"What do you want us to say to Mama and Father?" Arthur finally asked Albert.

"Leave that to me," Albert mumbled, "But if we just keep quiet, they will probably stay sleeping."

Nothing more was said. Soon Dolly pulled the wagon up beside the front porch and stopped. Arthur and Earl climbed down first, then gently helped Albert off the wagon. With a brother on each side, they quietly stepped up onto the porch. Arthur reached for the door just as barking started. "I thought you tied Shep up out back!" Arthur harshly whispered.

"I did!" Albert hissed.

Just then, the front door swung open and there stood Almon, holding a lit candle.

"Where have you three been?" he asked in a concerned voice as he held the candle closer to Albert. "And what happened to you?"

Albert quickly recited his prepared excuse. "I fell off the back of Top's wagon."

Almon held the candle closer yet, exposing Albert's bloodied knuckles. "Well, your mother may believe that . . . now go on and get off to bed."

Albert shuffled on in with Arthur's help while Shep followed. Earl turned to leave just as his father's voice asked, from behind, "Did he win?"

Earl slightly turned his head and nodded as he quietly said, "Yes."

CHAPTER 9

A Stolen Kiss at Memorial Day

May 30, 1917

The sunlight of a perfect day blanketed the area. Practically every house, every business, and every street pole displayed an American flag. A large crowd had gathered along both sides of the street. The 1:20 trolley had been halted just west of town to allow for a motorcade of white-daffodil-adorned black automobiles to pass through the elaborate display of flags. While the windblown flowers left a trail of white pedals, the flapping colors whirled ever stronger as the vehicles passed by. The band immediately fell in behind and started playing. The crowd filled the street as everyone began walking toward the cemetery to the strains of the band.

The Memorial Day ceremony lasted all afternoon with speeches, song, prayer, music, and recurring praises for the dwindling group of old war veterans who, like tin soldiers dressed in uniform, sat in a row on the makeshift platform. The chaplain sang his rendition of E.F. Stewart's song 'Cover Them Over with Beautiful Flowers' as younger veterans and soldiers decorated the graves of their fallen comrades-in-arms while the crowd looked on.

The band played George Fredrick Root's 'Battle Cry of Freedom' just before intermission. The band members dissolved into the crowd for the break. Earl flipped his trombone under his arm and made his way towards the refreshment table. When an opening appeared, he stepped in and leaned his instrument against the table's edge. He poured a cup of lemonade before turning to look at the surrounding crowd. All the talking was just muffled chatter in his ears as he took a second sip. Suddenly, a familiar voice called out from his right.

"Hello."

He lowered the cup from his lips and turned to look.

"Hello," he timidly replied.

Lucile immediately moved toward him. "It is so nice to see you," she smiled, while commenting, "I must say, the new band uniforms look great on all its members . . . especially you."

Earl was about to reply when he bumped his trombone and it began to slide from its perch. He dropped his cup and grabbed for the falling instrument as his drink splashed onto the lawn. A second seemed like an hour as he corralled the calamity. He glanced up to see that Lucile had stepped back to a safe distance.

Embarrassed, all he could say was, "Sorry."

Lucile smiled before stepping closer again and saying, "I wanted to ask . . ." She was instantly cut off by Everly Dane and his wife, Ruth, who suddenly emerged from the crowd. Not realizing Lucile was there, they stepped directly in front of her.

"How are you, Earl? It is good to see you!" Everly said as he enthusiastically grabbed Earl's free hand and shook it vigorously. He continued, "The band sounds wonderful. You members must be practicing a lot."

"Yes. I am sorry, but I must be going. . ." Earl said, hopefully excusing himself as he wrenched his neck, trying to see Lucile. Everly's next remark brought Earl's attention back. "I just talked to Albo. He told me all about that nasty fall he took off the back of your wagon."

"He did, did he?" Earl replied.

"Yes, but he looks to be healing up well. That is good, because I am going to need his and your help again soon. I want to plant that lower forty for the cause."

Earl threw on a quick smile and hastily replied, "Yes, yes. I must go now. It is wonderful to see both of you. I must go . . . I must leave now." He grabbed his instrument and darted behind the couple while grabbing Lucile's arm. He pulled her through the crowd and out of the Dane's view to the tree row that bordered the cemetery.

"My," Lucile stated as Earl stopped and released her arm. She straightened her hat while Earl leaned his trombone against the tree.

"I am sorry again," Earl said.

"You do not need to apologize." Lucile replied. She inquisitively asked, "But I am curious. What happened to your brother Albo?"

"Errr . . . he is fine. Now, what were you asking me before you were interrupted?"

Lucile hesitated and then said, "Why did you not come for my lesson last Thursday?"

Earl glanced away while saying, "I did not know if I was welcome anymore."

Lucile's mouth dropped. "Of course you are welcome! You have taught me more than any of my other instructors."

"Other instructors?" Earl loudly repeated as his eyes instantly locked on her.

"Why, yes. You could not have thought that anyone could advance as fast as I have without having had previous instruction."

Earl slowly shook his head as he turned away. He grabbed his trombone and started walking.

"Mr. Ames!" Lucile exclaimed. "Mr. Ames!"

Earl turned and shouted, "My name is Earl!

"Earl," she called out, a noticeable quiver in her voice.

Earl stopped. He could see the mist in her eyes.

He dropped his trombone and ran back, grabbed her hand, and pulled her behind the tree. Instantly, in pure emotion, they tightly embraced and kissed. The passion was so intense that the two slowly slid down the tree trunk. The continuous kiss went on until they were both on their knees.

Suddenly, Earl heard the band playing. He pulled away and spouted, "I must go!"

She momentarily stared into his blue eyes, and then he was gone. Lucile peeked from behind the tree just in time to see Earl, in full stride, grab his trombone from the ground and race to the band.

CHAPTER 10
Kill the Bull Before it Kills You

June 5, 1917

"Here it is," Almon said as he grabbed the newspaper off the tabletop. "They have been posting notices about this Registration Day for over a week, now." (Reported in the Titusville Hearld Newspaper on registration day, June 5, 1917, Page 4.) Almon unfolded the newspaper. The bold letters stared back as he paraphrased the news. "It says here that it is nationwide, and it is only today that those of age must register. If not, there is imprisonment of one year and then forced registration." Almon, in a dismayed manner, tossed the paper back onto the table while mumbling, "Your mother is already in the other room, hiding her tears from Clara." He looked Arthur directly in the eyes. "You must go to the home precinct. All I know is that it is down in Enterprise. Your Uncle John borrowed Prince yesterday, so he left his auto-car here. I suppose he will not mind you using it so you can get back quicker. Now, go get your Uncle Romey and Top. They will need to register, too."

Russell, Almon's younger son, spoke up. "Artie, I will go with you."

"You are only thirteen. Albert is too young, also," Almon said. "And besides, you have your and his chores to do today, since he is working that job up in Tidioute. I must leave here soon to go there myself."

"But I could help," Russell pleaded.

"Artie will do just fine. Now, get along. That hen house will not hoe itself out."

Russell turned and marched out of the room, slamming the door behind him. Because of his age, he always seemed alienated from his older brothers' adventures.

Almon turned back to Arthur. "If you hurry, you may yet have time today to get some work done."

"I will see you later," Arthur replied before heading for the door. He walked out to the four-door Model T that sat off to the side of the house. He had driven automobiles in the past, but not a lot. However, his Uncle John had taught him how to start one without breaking an arm—something that happened to people, on occasion, if the motor backfired. He looked inside to make sure the key was off and the tall handle was pulled back to the brake position. He flipped up the hood and turned on the fuel. He then closed the hood and moved to the front of the vehicle. He pulled the choke lever out and gave a quick pull up on the crank, priming the motor. He raced back and reached inside to turn on the key, then bolted back. He grabbed the crank with his left hand and gave a hard yank, then a second, and the motor started. He jumped inside and adjusted the throttle and spark advance levers on the steering column until the motor ran smoothly. He pulled the hand lever to the middle and stepped on the foot pedal and the auto began to move. He then pushed the hand lever completely forward, into overdrive.

A dust cloud spewed behind as Arthur drove the dirt road that followed the fence lines. He pulled up to McCamman's farm and set the brake. The motor ticked and rattled as he left the vehicle idling. He jumped out and went searching for Romey. He found him behind the barn, pitching manure into a wagon. "Hello, Uncle Romey."

"Artie! What brings you out here this forenoon?"

"We must register for the conscription today. I have your brother John's auto-car out front. Grab whatever you need and let us go."

"I cannot leave now. I have a lot to do, and I smell like cow dung."

"We must go, or you can face jail time. It probably will not take long. Father told me to pick up Top also."

Romey hesitated before reluctantly muttering, "All right." He jabbed his pitchfork into the manure pile to stand it there until he got back.

Soon, the two pulled up to Earl's barn. Arthur knew that Earl had planned on putting new shoes on Dolly today. Romey stayed with the vehicle as Arthur ran to the barn and threw open the barn door. "Top! You in here?" The commotion spooked Dolly and she jerked her leg away just as Earl was pounding in the last nail. "It is all right, girl," Earl consoled as he softly petted the horse. "I am back here," he called out to Arthur.

Arthur walked back to the stall just as Earl was gently lifting Dolly's hind leg again. "Here, Artie, help me finish this."

Arthur stepped into the stall and straddled Dolly's leg. In a moment, Earl had the last nail pounded in. Earl took Dolly's leg from Arthur and finished the task by running a file over the hoof and shoe. "How do they feel, Dolly?" he said after he set her leg down. The horse noticed the difference and subtly pranced. "If need be, I will adjust them for you later, old girl," Earl then looked at Arthur.

"I think you know why I am here," Arthur said.

"Yes," is the only word Earl used in response as he tossed the file into his wooden toolbox.

"I have Uncle John's auto-car out front. Let us go."

Earl grabbed the box and set it outside the stall. He looked back to the horse just before pulling off his denim apron and hanging it on a nearby nail. The two brothers exited the barn.

The ride to Enterprise did not take long. The place they were going to was highly visible. A large sign hung above the doors of the building, with large letters reading 'WAR REGISTRATION PRECINCT, JUNE 5, 1917, 7AM TO 9PM.' An American flag flew above the sign. There was a long line of men waiting for their turn to fill out the required paperwork.

Arthur parked and then Romey, Earl, and he took their place in the line. Step by step, they moved closer. They were just at the door when Jack Litzinger came walking out. "Jack!" Arthur called out.

Jack stepped over. "Hello, fellows!" he enthusiastically remarked as his defiant youth revealed itself in his rhetoric. "Can you believe this? Today puts us all one step closer to the battle. I cannot wait to be dressed up as a soldier boy and kill some Huns!"

The other three looked on with indifference painted on their faces.

"Then why have you not enlisted already?" Arthur finally asked.

"Well," Jack stumbled while his mind conjured up a response, "my parents do want me to stay home for a while, yet, because they need help on the farm."

"All right." Arthur accepted that statement as truer than the previous condescending remarks.

Jack thought a moment longer before replying, "Well, Artie, come to think of it, I just decided that I am going to enlist next month. That way, I have a lot better chance of not missing out on the fight. Now, I have work to do. Nice seeing you, fellows." Jack walked away.

The line moved just after Jack left, and soon it was Arthur, Romey, and Earl's turn to step before the clerks. The first clerk asked their names before handing each a registration card. The second clerk handed them pencils while pointing to a line of tables. "You can fill this out over there."

The three sat down and answered the questions. Lastly, they tossed their pencils into a bucket before handing the filled-out cards to a man stationed by the door. "Thank you," the man said as he gave each of them a copy.

As the three walked back to the automobile together, Earl seemed burdened by what had just taken place. Arthur sensed his brother's uneasiness and consoled, "Do not be concerned, Top. It is just the registration part. The war will probably be over before we get called up."

Earl slightly shook his head and said, "I have reached the edge of a dream. I hope I have the time to make it come true."

Arthur, not understanding what Earl was referring to, remarked, "If it is that old crisscross log fence that you have been forever talking about repairing … well, you got time."

Back at home, Russell was still upset over doing all the chores.

His father had said to hoe out the hen house. He decided to protest, and weeded the garden first. The thin teenager worked away until he finally stood with the last handful of weeds. He threw them as hard as he could, but they barely left the garden before fluttering to the ground. "I am doomed to doing chores the rest of my life," he mumbled as he walked to the coop. He kicked at the pen door to scare the chickens back. The hens seemed to be clucking in protest themselves, as they scattered. He quickly opened the door and closed it behind him before grabbing the hoe that leaned against the chicken wire. He stepped inside and began scraping the wooden floor as his anger and the hot musty coop caused his sandy brown hair to curl from his sweat.

Clara had walked to her grandmother's house, and Russell was too far away to hear the frantic knock on the house door. Shep, startled from his sleep, jumped up and began barking. The calamity sent Ella running for the door. She yanked it open to see Ruth Dane standing there, shaking. Terror was strewn across her face as tears ran down her cheeks. "Please! Please!" she pleaded. "I need help quick! The bull is attacking Everly! It has him pinned behind the wood pile in the corral!"

Ella immediately pushed past Ruth and ran to the backyard. Shep ran with her. "Russell! Russell!" she screamed.

Russell heard his name being called. He stopped hoeing and looked out of the coop to see his mother running his way. The fear in her voice was startling, "Come quick! Everly is being attacked by his bull!"

Russell knew that bull's reputation. He dropped his hoe and ran for the house. Shep followed and slipped in behind him when Russell yanked open the back door. He darted to the kitchen and jerked a drawer open to retrieve the 45-caliber handgun. He grabbed a handful of cartridges and stuffed them in his pocket and darted back outside. The door slammed, imprisoning Shep inside.

The two women and Russell ran across the fields to Dane's farm. Along the way, Ruth shouted out the story of how Everly had gone into the barn to feed the horse when the bull got loose and chased them both into the corral. The horse was quicker, and the bull rammed Everly from behind, knocking him down before trampling and goring him. Everly had managed to crawl behind the wood pile when the bull went after the horse.

Profusely panting, the women and Russell finally reached the corral. Everything seemed eerily quiet. There was no sign of the bull and the horse was out at the far fence, just standing there. The women stood back, holding each other in fear as Russell cautiously approached the corral's fence. "Russell, be careful," his mother hissed as he climbed over the top rail. As he lowered himself down, all Russell could hear was his racing heart and his rapid breathing. His eyes darted back and forth before he looked to the ground to see a single boot lying among a multitude of erratic scuffs, hoof prints, and patches of splattered blood—evidence of a great scuffle. With hands shaking, he cautiously continued toward the wood pile that leaned against the back of the barn. It was then, that he spied a foot barely sticking out from behind the wood. He hurried over, knelt, and peered into the small opening between the barn wall and the wood. In the dingy light, he could make out a bloodied figure with torn clothes lying face down. "Mr. Dane! Mr. Dane!" Russell sharply whispered. He touched Everly's leg, instantly, moans came from the man. He was still alive.

Suddenly, something aroused the bull and it came out of the barn. Not noticing Russell crouched by the wood, the bull seen the horse and charged. The horse began snorting. It kicked the ground with its hoofs in warning as the bull approached. A chase instantly ensued as both animals began running in circles. The horse kicked with each leap as it bellowed in fear, while the bull followed closely behind. Suddenly, the animals turned straight toward Russell. Gun in hand, Russell jumped behind a nearby pole that stood in the corral. The horse, with both back legs, kicked the bull in the face just as they whisked past Russell. The bull felt the brunt of the kick and slowed to a trot while shaking its head. The horse cut left, in full gallop, and ran into the barn.

The bull then noticed Russell, and immediately charged. "RUSSELL!" Ella screamed as Ruth restrained her from running into the corral.

From behind the pole, Russell held out the gun with his right hand and fired. Boom! Boom! Boom! Did he miss? The bull was almost on him! He frantically shot again. Boom! Boom! The hair flew from the animal's brisket as the second bullet ripped through the beast's jaw. The bull whirled and trotted back as it snorted and gurgled in the blood that ran from its mouth. Russell nervously clicked open the gun and shook out the spent casings. His quivering hand reached in his pocket for more ammunition, but he fumbled the cartridges and they tumbled to the ground. He dropped to his knees, scraping his fingers through the dirt, jamming any bullet he found into the gun. Just then, the bull regained its composure and charged again. With no time to climb behind the pole, Russell slammed the gun shut and knelt. He aimed and fired. Boom! Boom! Boom! Three hits, but the beast was still coming. Russell leapt to one side just as the bull reached him, and rolled to his feet. He fired the last two shots into the animal's neck just as it passed by. The beast stumbled a bit farther and stopped. With labored, gurgled breathing, the blood bubbled from the animal's wounds as it stood for what seemed like eternity . . . it then collapsed to the ground.

Hands shaking, Russell scratched through the dirt to find one more bullet. He slammed it into the gun and cautiously approached the beast. He held the gun directly on the animal as he quickly kicked it once, then twice. No movement. It was dead.

Ruth and Ella immediately threw open the gate and ran for the wood pile. Russell dropped his gun and followed. They pulled Everly's tattered body from his refuge and rolled him over. The man's hair was soaked in blood, which also covered his face, from a large gash. His clothes were ripped to shreds. Among all the other scrapes and bruises was a puncture wound flowing blood from his side. Ruth pulled off her apron and ripped it in strips. "Russell, help us roll him again!" Ella commanded.

They bound the terrible hole in Everly's side. Ella yelled to Russell again. "Run to Hoffbauer's. Tell them what has happened, and have them bring their auto-car!"

Russell immediately took off, and soon Mr. Hoffbauer was pulling into the corral. The group lifted Everly to his feet. As they struggled to get him into Hoffbauer's vehicle, Everly caught site of the bull's carcass and cried out, "He killed my bull, Ruth . . . he killed my bull."

Everly was still chanting those words as they laid him across the back seat. Ruth jumped into the passenger side as Mr. Hoffbauer let the clutch out and drove to Doc Proper's.

CHAPTER 11

The Fair and the Parade for First Draftees

September 10, 1917

S pring and summer seemed to only be days long. September, with its cooler evenings, sweet smells, and occasional streaks of color peeking through the leaves, had begun to claim the season. Legends of the fall harvest from previous times could not compare to the dramatic increase in crop production brought on by the U.S. Food Administration's campaign, "Food Will Win The War." This was the request for American farmers to grow more.

Everyone was also encouraged to follow the other programs of "Meatless Mondays" and "Wheatless Wednesdays" to conserve for the war effort. America was not only feeding its own people and soldiers but also helping to feed Europe, where the war had devastated agricultural production. Many European farmers had become soldiers or casualties, and thousands of acres of farmland were either destroyed or turned into battlefields.

Amidst the constant war cry, life carried on in its own ways. Lucile was still learning the piano with Earl. With the emotional stress of their earlier meetings seemingly lessened, she had progressed considerably and rarely stumbled. She had just finished one piece when, out of nowhere, she turned to Earl and said, "I saw your brother Albert today. He had a terrible black eye and scratches on his face. He told me he had fallen off the back of your wagon again." Earl shook his head in disbelief as Lucile continued, "You are his older brother. You must council him on being more careful. When I told Mother, she was appalled."

Earl, wanting to end the charade, instantly asked, "Have you heard of jazz?"

"I have heard the word, but have never listened to any."

Earl hesitated, then looked around to see where Lucile's mother was. "All right," he said, "it is time you heard some. I have been working on this piece by the Evergreen Classic Jazz Band called, 'Stomp Off, Let's Go.'" Earl immediately commenced playing the brash music, toned down at first. But as Lucile began to clap along, Earl cranked up the volume. He leaned back with a big smile and beat the keys harder.

Suddenly Lucile's mother stepped into the room and banged her cane on the floor. "Stop it! Stop that wretched noise!" she angrily announced. The piano fell silent as Eleanor continued, "We will not have that kind of music in this house!" She stared at the couple and then walked away.

Lucile and Earl sat quietly on the piano bench until Lucile whispered, "I did not think that music would affect her so."

"Why did it?" Earl whispered back.

Lucile responded, "She thinks that certain things are below us."

Earl did not respond to Lucile's answer, and immediately changed the subject. "The Titusville Fair starts tomorrow. The band is playing, so, I will not be here on Thursday. I thought . . . you might come with me?"

Lucile hesitated before saying, "I will meet you there."

The lesson ended and the two parted ways.

The first day of the fair did not bring much of a crowd. The Pleasantville Band and other bands played to a sparsely populated grandstand. At each intermission, Earl searched the crowd, hoping to find Lucile, but she was not there. The crowds grew each day, and each day Lucile did not show. Earl noticed that Albert had not shown up, either. Each time Earl had asked Arthur; he received the same answer: "Albo did not come today."

By Friday, Earl played to intermission. His patience had been pushed too far. The moment the last song ended, he hurried over to Arthur and asked, in a stern voice, "Where is Albo?"

"He did not come today," Arthur automatically replied.

"I can see that," Earl spouted.

Just then, the band leader, Mr. Watson, came over to the two brothers, interrupting their conversation by saying, "Hello boys." He immediately singled out Earl. "I am so sorry to hear of Albert falling off of the back of your wagon again."

Earl stood silent, unable to respond as Mr. Watson continued, "I hope he is healed up by next week. The band has been invited to Titusville to lead the Conscription Parade celebration for all the men leaving for the service, and we need him as first trumpet. Since Jack Litzinger joined the army, we have been weak, there. It is next Tuesday, the nineteenth. We will meet at the Methodist Church and take the 4 o'clock trolley to Titusville. Please tell him."

"I certainly will," Arthur interjected. "He will be fine by then."

"Well, good. Now, I must go. I want to get a piece of Mrs. Smith's wonderful cherry pie before we play again."

As Mr. Watson walked away, Earl's eyes flashed back to Arthur. "Now, is it two times, or three, that he has fallen off the back of my wagon?"

"Two . . . well, maybe three," Arthur responded.

Earl shook his head in disbelief before saying, "I will deal with Albo when I see him, but I cannot worry about that right now. Here, take my horn until I get back."

"Where are you going?"

"To Pleasantville."

"But we have to play again in an hour."

"I will be back," Earl said as he shoved his trombone into Arthur's hands and began to leave. Earl suddenly turned back and asked, "Did he win?"

"Yes," Arthur replied with a smile. Earl dashed away. He hopped the two o'clock trolley to Pleasantville. As he made his way down the aisle, an occasional person would look at his uniform and smile in admiration, but recently, more faces seemed to look with indifference. Earl took an empty seat and soon stepped off on Main Street, Pleasantville. He ran to Lucile's house and knocked at her door. Lucile's mother Eleanor answered.

"Hello, Mrs. Lake," Earl said with a forced smile while noticing the disenchantment on her face.

"Lucile has the flu today," Eleanor replied with insensitivity.

Earl momentarily stood, staring at her, before responding, "Well, tell her I hope she gets to feeling better."

Eleanor only gave a nod and closed the door.

Earl slowly turned from the door and walked to the trolley, confused. Was Eleanor telling the truth? Or was he being rejected?

The desire to return to the fair was not in his heart, but there seemed to be no other choice. Earl returned in time, and played with the band through the rest of the fair. He was back pumping his leases and working on his farm, afterwards.

Tuesday came. The band loaded onto the 4 o'clock trolley from Pleasantville to Titusville. Just as it was about to leave, a last band member hurried on. Earl shook his head as Albert traipsed down the aisle and took the seat next to Earl. Albert instantly blurted out, "I won!"

"I know, Albo," Earl responded. "Artie told me."

Albert looked at Earl, expecting a lecture. Instead, Earl said, "Do me a favor, Albo. The next time you need an excuse, say you fell off someone else's wagon."

Albert gave a big smile of relief and replied, "I must come up with a different excuse. That one seems to be wearing out. Even Mama is starting to wonder. Hey, can I borrow Dolly next time?"

"No!"

The conversation continued for the rest of the ride as Albert narrated every moment of his bout. When the trolley came into town, the story ended. The two brothers peered out of the trolley window, noticing that all the businesses were closed and decorated, along with almost all the houses. Citizens already lined the sidewalks on every street the trolley traveled.

The ride ended on Franklin Street. Onlookers stared at the spectacle of a twenty-two-piece band, in full uniform, carrying their instruments, unloading from a trolley. The parade would start there.

Soon, the procession was lined up. Automobiles carrying Grand Marshall Doctor W. G. Johnston and his aides led the way. Next was the Pleasantville Band in all their grandeur, loudly playing patriotic songs. Just behind them were the Titusville area's first fifty-eight conscripted men, who received enthusiastic, spontaneous cheers from the crowd lining the streets. The local war veterans, along with the Woman's Relief Corps, rode in decorated autos, followed by a flatbed truck with side rails, designated for throwing money and tobacco products to the recruits. Those who had the least gave the most. The vehicle was guarded by fifteen Boy Scouts, who made sure everything thrown got onto the truck. William Tinsley's twelve-piece drum corps followed, creating lively martial music. After that came five hundred of Titusville's high school students, each carrying an American flag. Just behind them were three hundred parochial school students, also carrying flags. The fraternal organizations of Elks, Knights of Columbus, and Eagles members followed, along with local businessmen. Autos carrying the Red Cross nurses came afterward. Thirty Titusville firemen, dressed in full uniform, escorted two horse-drawn hose wagons, bringing up the rear.

The parade came to an end at the YMCA, where a dinner had been prepared by the women of the YWCA for the draftees and dignitaries.

Earl was standing on the sidewalk, taking in the site of the crowd, when Arthur came over. "Did you hear what Mr. Watson just announced?"

"No."

"A group of Titusville businessmen are buying supper for our band at the Mansion House. Follow me. We are storing our instruments in the YMCA coat room."

"Where is Albo?"

"Did you notice that I am carrying his horn and mine? I sent him ahead to save us a table."

"All right," Earl replied as he and Arthur stepped in line to leave their instruments.

The disbanding parade swelled the crowd on the sidewalks even more. Arthur and Earl slowly made their way through an ocean of humanity until they reached the upscale restaurant and hotel. Upon entering, the chatter of dozens of voices filled the air, along with the sight of all the patrons and the tantalizing aromas of prepared food. Immediately, Albert caught their attention by wildly flailing his arms. Earl and Arthur made their way over and sat down. They both tossed their hats on the table as Albert muttered, "Can you believe this? We are taking supper at the Mansion House. We have made it, brothers. They have waitresses, who are total strangers, come to your table and ask what you want to eat. Then they bring your food to you, just like Mama."

Earl and Arthur both snickered just as a waitress came to their table and handed them menus.

With the food served, all three brothers were quietly eating when Arthur struck up a conversation. "I talked to Mr. Hoffbauer the other day. He said that Everly Dane has one of the Dykins boys doing the farm chores, since he still cannot get around after that bull attack. Hoffbauer also said that Everly is still upset about Russell shooting his prize bull, so he bought two bull calves."

"Why would he do that?" Albert spoke up. "His farm is too small. He will have to keep them separated when they get older, or most likely they will be fighting."

Arthur added, "He told Mr. Hoffbauer that he wanted two, just in case an Ames boy came over and shot one."

Albert dropped his fork onto his plate. He shook his head while sarcastically remarking, "He does not appreciate that Russell saved his life! There was no other choice. Everly would have bled to death before anyone could have corralled that animal."

Earl glanced across the room to see if anyone had noticed Albo's outburst. Along with band member uniforms sticking out everywhere in the crowd, he glimpsed three people sitting at a secluded table in the corner. He squinted and recognized two of them.

Earl stood up, to the amazement of his brothers. Immediately, Arthur asked, "Where are you going, Top?"

Earl never heard Arthur, as his mind was trained on the people in the corner. As if in a trance, he walked straight through the crowd until he was standing directly in front of them. All three looked up just as Earl said, "Hello."

"Why, nice to see you, Earl," Lucile politely said. She continued, "You already know my mother."

Earl politely nodded with a reserved smile as Eleanor stared at him.

Lucile said, "Father, this is my piano tutor, Mr. Earl Ames."

Lucile's father stood and shook Earl's hand while saying, "The name is Grant. Grant Lake. Nice to meet you."

"Nice to meet you sir," Earl responded as his mind raced. *Where has he been all this time?*

An awkward silence commenced until Earl asked, "Lucile, is our lesson on for this Thursday?"

"Yes."

Earl noticed Eleanor's body language and instantly said, "Well, I must go. It was nice meeting you, Mr. Lake . . . Mrs. Lake . . . Lucile."

Earl turned and walked away with what seemed to him to be every eye in the restaurant watching. He walked over to Albert and Arthur and grabbed his hat while saying, "I am going to go get my trombone. I will see you two later."

Arthur, oblivious to what had just taken place, asked, "You are not going to finish your meal?"

"No, I have to go."

Albert spoke up. "I am finishing it for you, then."

"I get some, too," Arthur interjected.

The two brothers began splitting up Earl's food as he walked out the door. Earl put on his hat and made his way through the thinning crowd as questions filled his mind. *Why did she introduce me as just 'the piano tutor'? Why is Eleanor jilting me?*

He reached the YMCA and went inside to retrieve his trombone just as the Honorable John L. Emerson of the draft board was giving an impassioned speech. Earl stood in the coat closet, listening to Mr. Emerson's words. "You have only honor and affection in our hearts," he proclaimed, "You are to fight our battles so that it will be safer, in the future, for democracy. I wish you Godspeed on your trip, and a safe and speedy return. May God grant that this is so."

A large applause erupted before the audience broke into song.

A couple of veterans, dressed in uniform, walked into the coat room. They were in deep conversation and never acknowledged Earl standing there. One veteran stated, "We never got a sendoff like this."

The second man replied, "Because of the conscription, they are the first to go, that is not of their choosing. I am certain those who follow will never be acknowledged like this."

"I just hope and pray they all come back alive, and in one piece," the first man said.

The two grabbed their overcoats and walked past Earl as if he still did not exist. Earl picked up his horn and left. He boarded the next trolley to Pleasantville and went home.

CHAPTER 12

Searching for Sugar with a High-Strung Horse

November 1917

"I am truly sorry, Mrs. Ames," the grocer sincerely replied. "I have had to apologize to almost every patron that comes through the door. We have had sugar on order from our supplier for well over a month now, and still we receive none." (Reported in the Titusville Hearld Newspaper, November 13, 1917, Page 2.)

"I have checked with the grocers in Enterprise and Pleasantville," Ella responded. "They have no sugar, either. That is why I had my son drive me to Titusville. I felt that, being a much larger town, there would surely be sugar to purchase. I have Thanksgiving Dinner to start baking for, soon. What will it be like without sugar in the recipes?"

"I understand," the grocer said, shaking his head. "With so many ships being diverted to haul supplies to the war front and Europe's sugar crop mostly destroyed, it seems that we here at home have been made to sacrifice. I know it is of little comfort, but President Wilson moving Thanksgiving to the 29th because of an extra Thursday in November this year gives everyone a little more time to figure out what to do."

Ella looked at the grocer and replied, "Well, thank you for your time, Mr. Anderson."

Ella had turned to leave when the grocer called out, "Wait."

She glanced back as Mr. Anderson said, "You might try Fenton's grocery over in the Brunswick Block. I have heard that they received a partial shipment. But I am told that they are only selling one pound to each customer, trying to accommodate as many patrons as possible."

"Thank you again, Mr. Anderson," Ella replied. "I will do that."

Ella walked out to Earl and Dolly, who were waiting with the buggy. She climbed up and said, "Take us to the Brunswick Block. Fenton's grocery may have some sugar."

"Yes, Mama," Earl replied as he flicked the reins. "Let us go, Dolly."

The horse eased the wagon out onto the busy thoroughfare, only to have a trolley suddenly appear from a side street. The abrupt presence of the noisy machine startled Dolly. She braced her neck upward as her ears pointed directly at the trolley. Earl could hear her heavy breathing as she gave out a neigh. He immediately put steady tension on the reins and, in a calming manner, said, "Easy, girl, easy."

The horse stood erect, staring at the approaching trolley. Suddenly she reared up on her hind legs, arched her neck back, and lunged left. The whites of her eyes flashed as she loudly neighed again while yanking the buggy mercilessly sideways. People jumped from the way as Ella dropped to the buggy seat, tightly hugging it with both arms. Earl was tossed about as the rig spun in a wild circle. The horse charged down the street, zigzagging at full gallop between vehicles, other horses, and people. Earl regained enough balance to yank back the brake lever, but that only locked the rear wheels, causing the buggy to violently skid back and forth. Earl flipped off the brake and pulled on the reins again, while frantically shouting, "Whoa, Dolly! Whoa, girl! Whoa!" Dolly ignored the command and continued at full gallop. She shook her head fiercely, fighting the bit in her mouth.

Earl glanced ahead to see the street blocked by a stopped truck on one side and a line of automobiles on the other. He had to do something. He yanked the right rein with all his might, violently jerking Dolly's head far back to the side. Earl's action caused the horse to rear up on her hind legs as her hoofs skidded on the brick street. Dolly almost fell before making the abrupt turn. The buggy skidded broadside and onto the side street. Still snorting and shaking her head, Dolly returned to full gallop as Earl planted both feet and pulled again on the reins with every ounce of his strength. The force slowed the horse to a trot before she finally stopped.

Earl pulled the brake lever again before cautiously easing back on the reins. He called out, "Mama! Mama! Are you all right?"

"I think so," Ella replied as she let go of the seat and sat up. She was shaking as she adjusted her bonnet, and tried to calmly say, "I thought I was going to be thrown off."

Earl never waited to finish hearing Ella's remark as he climbed from the wagon and cautiously approached Dolly. The horse was still breathing heavily. "You are all right, girl, you are all right," he consoled as he delicately put his hand on Dolly's side. The horse flinched at his touch. Ever so lightly he slowly slid his hand ahead to the animal's neck. The sweat was still pouring from the horse as he then gently stroked Dolly's mane. In a soothing voice, he said, "You scared us, girl. You are all right now. You are safe."

Dolly was still shaking, but was starting to calm. Earl slid his hand down Dolly's legs, rib cage, and hind quarters to make sure the horse was not injured. He then put his cheek to Dolly's, and closed his eyes, while lightly petting her and gently whispering. Suddenly he heard his mother loudly hiss, "Top! There are people coming!"

Earl glanced behind to see a herd of sightseers and good Samaritans rushing toward Ella and him. He hurriedly moved back to the buggy, jumped up into the seat, unlocked the brake and flicked the reins. Dolly instantly responded to his command and began to trot.

"We will be all right now," Earl said reassuringly.

"I just want to go home," Ella responded.

Earl understood and said nothing as he steered Dolly and the buggy towards home. They followed the back roads, away from the trolleys.

After they had traveled a ways, the sun's rays momentarily broke out from the overcast sky. A slight breeze lifted a few fallen leaves from alongside the road and sent them scurrying in front of Dolly. Those dancing leaves seemed to help Ella find the courage to say something that was bothering her. "Thank God we are all uninjured," she remarked as she grabbed the lap blanket from behind the seat and spread it across Earl and herself.

"Yes," Earl replied.

The sun hid behind the gray clouds again just as a few snowflakes began to gently float in the air. Ella conjured up her courage once more and continued, "This horse of yours is so high-strung, why did you chance bringing her instead of Prince?"

Earl said nothing as Ella added, "And another thing ... I am certain that this is the completely wrong time to talk about it, but while I am in this mood I must say that I have been told that you are fond of that girl you are giving piano lessons to—the Lakes' daughter. I hear she is very pretty."

Earl said nothing.

Ella resumed, "Well, I am going to just come out and say it . . . I think you should reconsider, if you are thinking of courting this girl."

"Why would you say such a thing, Mama?" Earl spouted in surprise.

Ella continued, "It is hard for me to tell you this, my son, but the Lakes have a far different background from us. They have money, and come from the city. Our family has lived in these backwoods for generations. I am sure she is a fine girl, but most likely she would never find happiness in our way of life."

"I see nothing wrong with our way of life. Why would she have trouble with it?"

"Earl Leslie!" Ella sternly spouted before calming herself to resume talking. "Son, she is not of our kind . . . I am only thinking of you when I say this. A person must safeguard their heart. A broken heart can only bring sorrow and regret."

Earl stayed silent and stared straight ahead as Dolly's hoofs clip-clopped on the road and gravel crackled under the buggy's rolling wheels.

The sky was spitting snow when they reached Ella's house. Earl pulled the rig up close to the front porch and brought Dolly to a halt.

Ella looked at her son as he still stared straight ahead. "Earl, what I have said is out of my love for you. I will accept whatever choice you make . . . now, I want you to come to dinner on Thanksgiving. I still do not know what it may taste like."

"I will, Mama," Earl replied as he climbed off the buggy and helped his mother to the door. Ella turned and gave her son a large hug while saying, "Take care, my eldest."

Earl nodded goodbye and walked back to the buggy. On his way home, his mind dwelled on his mother's opinion and how his chances of courting Lucile seemed to dim almost every time he saw her.

Two days later, Earl was at band practice when his brother Albert came up to him. "Hello, Albo," Earl said jovially.

"Hello, Top," Albert replied. "Just wanted to let you know that I got Mama some sugar;"

"How?"

Pumped up with pride, Albert remarked, "A few stores in Centerville still had some, so I called in a favor I was owed and got five pounds."

"I am so happy."

"So am I."

CHAPTER 13
Thanksgiving Turmoil before an Audition

Late November 1917

Lucile played Erik Satie's "Gymnopedies" until the last note echoed from the piano. She then sat silent on the bench alongside Earl.

"Excellent," Earl said. "Soon you will not need my help anymore."

Astonished by the comment, Lucile looked at Earl and spoke up. "But I am not as good as you. You play with such feeling, such emotion—how does a person learn that?"

"You have learned the basics," Earl replied. "With what you already knew from your previous tutors, you have advanced quickly. Soon it will be just practice and learning new pieces. But to find the emotion in music, you must reach inside. . . feel every note. At times I close my eyes and become one with the sound. The emotion is there. If you reach with your soul, you will find it."

"I cannot close my eyes to play. I would never find the right keys."

"You can." Earl replied. "When I was young, I learned when my Mama taught me. We used to practice late in the evening by candlelight. I could barely see the keys, so I would close my eyes and feel them. You can do this."

Lucile immediately ended the topic by stating, "But, I need yo— . . .." she stopped short of what she was about to say.

Earl picked up on her vulnerability and blurted out something he had previously decided was too forward. "Next Thursday is

Thanksgiving. I will not be here . . . would you accompany me to my parents' home for Thanksgiving dinner?"

Lucile was stymied. She thought before responding. "My parents and I have little family here, so we plan to go to the seven o'clock church service."

"Then it is settled!" Earl blurted out. "I will pick you up at eleven and have you back before church begins."

Lucile had to think fast. Immediately, she responded, "I will meet you at the town square."

Earl reeled on the news that Lucile had agreed, but a perplexed expression crossed his face before he said, "All right . . . I will be at the town square at eleven."

Afterward, Earl went home, did his chores, and then wrote his mother about the guest he was bringing to Thanksgiving. Ella would receive the letter the following day.

Thanksgiving Day came. Earl put on his best suit, overcoat, hat, and sheepskin gloves. He hooked Dolly to the buggy and headed to town. As he entered its outskirts, he noticed the sidewalks were almost devoid of people. During his trip, only a few vehicles had passed by. The stores were closed, as most people were with their families for the Thanksgiving meal, or in church.

Earl squinted hard to see the town square as it came into sight. There! He could make out the silhouette of someone sitting on a bench. He flipped the reins and Dolly trotted a little faster.

"Whoa," Earl said as he brought the rig to a stop at the square. He climbed off the buggy and walked over to where she sat. Lucile was dressed in a long green winter coat with a wide fur collar. Matching fur striped the tops of her boots, and her contrasting felt hat was adorned with an ostrich plume which complimented the hand muff nuzzled in her lap. She looked like a princess. She flashed her silver-blue eyes at him as he said, "Hello." Lucile smiled as Earl continued, "It is so wonderful to see you." He cordially held out his hand, which she took as she stood. The sight of her looking up directly at him overwhelmed Earl as he remarked, "You look beautiful."

"Thank you," Lucile replied. "You look debonair."

The two stood looking at each other. Earl wanted to kiss her, but hesitated, feeling that move was too forward. "Shall we go?" he finally replied.

Lucile said nothing as Earl led her to the buggy. He assisted her onto the seat and then jumped up and pulled a lap blanket over them both.

He flicked the reins and Dolly began pulling the buggy around the square and back up the street. The sounds of the wheels rolling along and Dolly's hoofs clomping was all that broke the silence until a few snowflakes lazily floated down from the gray sky. "Messengers from above," Earl announced as some of the flakes landed on the lap blanket.

Lucile examined the miniature hexagon shapes and remarked, "They look like tiny crystals."

"At times, it seems as if those points on the snowflakes are sharp enough to stab, when a person is freezing. But, be it today or weeks from now, their message is always true: the snow *will* come to blanket the ground."

Lucile hesitated, then giggled and said, "Your descriptions of the obvious are so innocent."

Earl could only smile, but that response seemed to lay a foundation for a true conversation that developed. The two talked of many things as Dolly pulled the buggy along. Earl finally asked, "What did your parents say about you going with me today?"

Lucile casually remarked, "I did not tell them."

The answer stymied Earl. He immediately questioned, "Where do they think you are?"

"I told them I was going to my girlfriend Elizabeth's for Thanksgiving dinner."

Earl had no idea what to say as his mind kept repeating, *She is here with me, she is here with me, that is all that matters.* He dropped the topic.

Dolly knew exactly where to go when they arrived at Ella's and Almon's home. She pulled the buggy up to the hitching post and stopped. Immediately, the dog on the porch jumped up and began to bark. "Shep has announced our presence," Earl said as he stepped down from the buggy. Dolly had already found the water trough and had her head in it as Earl tied the reins to the post. He walked around and helped Lucile down, but as they started toward the house, she pushed him ahead while asking, "Does the dog bite?"

"Shep?" Earl questioned, "No, he is all bark."

The couple stepped onto the porch and immediately Shep began wagging his tail so hard that his whole body shook. Earl knelt and the dog jumped into his arms and licked Earl's face. When Earl finally stood, Shep scooted behind him to welcome Lucile. She immediately jerked away. "All right, Shep," Earl said. "Lucile needs time to get used to you." The dog seemed to understand, and backed off.

Just then, the door opened and there stood Ella. She was dressed in her best apron and a large smile was on her face as she gave a big hug to Earl while saying, "Top, I am so happy you are here. Happy Thanksgiving."

"Happy Thanksgiving to you, Mama," Earl responded.

Ella stepped back, waiting for what she knew was coming.

Earl blurted out, "Mama, this is Lucile."

The smile left Ella's face as she glared at Lucile, who was looking out from behind Earl.

"It is nice to meet you, Mrs. Ames. Happy Thanksgiving." Lucile then presented a shy smile.

Ella nodded back and mumbled, "Hello."

An awkward moment ensued until Ella backed away from blocking the doorway and said, "Come on in. The rest of the family is already here. I have set another plate." She held the door for the couple. The dog was right behind when Ella said, "Shep, you will have to stay out. There are too many people in this small house, and you may trip someone. I will bring you a treat later." Shep seemed discouraged as he watched Ella close the door. He then retreated to his favorite place on the porch.

Lucile glanced around at the small front room as Earl took her coat and hat and draped them across the divan along with his. The two walked to the dining area. The welcome was much warmer for Lucile when she entered the room and met Earl's brothers and his father. Arthur and Albert remembered her and gave her warm greetings, as if Lucile was an old friend. Russell was mesmerized by her beauty, while Almon showed a friendly smile as he introduced himself. Little Clara stared at Lucile. She finally said, "I am Clara."

"How are you, Clara?" Lucile responded in a sweet voice.

"I am fine. . . You are pretty."

Lucile blushed as she smiled. Suddenly, Ella came from the kitchen with an apron in her hand. She walked over to Lucile and said, "I need help serving."

"Mama!" Earl spouted, "Lucile is a guest!"

Lucile immediately touched Earl's arm. He looked at her as her eyes spoke *sit down*. Lucile politely took the apron and stood before following Ella to the kitchen. Just as the two women left the room, Almon looked around at everyone. They all knew what he was saying by the look in his eyes. Clara and the men stood in unison and walked to the kitchen. They carried every plate of the great feast to the table.

Lucile kept the apron on during the meal, and was the first one to stand afterward to gather dirty dishes. Ella immediately did the same, acting as if she would not be outdone by another woman. Everyone went into the kitchen again to help, but they were shushed away by Ella.

Ella poured hot water from a kettle sitting on the stove into a tub full of dishes and began instructing Lucile on how to wash them. The two women washed in complete silence. Once they were done, Lucile took off the apron, laid it at the edge of the sink, and walked back to the dining room. Ella looked out from the kitchen with a blank look on her face. Seeing his mother's and Lucile's expressions, Earl immediately stood and said, "Well, we must go. Thank you, Mama, for the great meal."

Everyone began saying goodbye as Lucile continued to the front room and grabbed her coat and hat. She was already pulling on her garments when Earl came into the room. He grabbed his coat and hat just as Lucile exited out the front door. Shep jumped up and wagged his tail, but Lucile ignored him as she walked to the buggy and climbed in. Earl was right behind her. Shep watched in confusion as Earl quickly untied the reins from the hitching post and jumped into the buggy. "Let us go, Dolly," he said as he flicked the reins.

The ride began without conversation until Earl said, "I am truly sorry for what happened."

"Why does your mother hate me?" Lucile blurted.

"She does not hate you … she is just old fashioned. If we go there again, I will make sure Mama does not ask you to do anything."

Lucile charged, "It is not *what* she asked me to do . . . it is *how* she asked me. She made me feel degraded and she insinuated that I have never served or did dishes, before."

Nothing more was said, and the couple rode on until Earl commanded, "Whoa." Dolly halted the buggy in front of an old house.

"Why are we stopping here?" Lucile asked.

"This is my farm," Earl proudly responded as he flipped the reins and Dolly pulled the buggy up to the front porch steps. "I want you to see it."

Earl jumped from the buggy before helping Lucile down. The two walked into the little house. Earl grabbed a twig from the tender box, opened the door of the stove, and lit it from the glowing coals. He darted around in the twilight, lighting all three of his kerosene lamps. The glow of the lamps now showed the room.

Lucile could see his upright piano, sheets of music neatly stacked on the instrument's shelf. There was an old rocker and a wooden-armed sofa, to one side. A small drop-leaf table with two chairs sat adjacent to the hand pump sink. She said nothing as Earl grabbed one of the lamps, took her hand, and led her to the other rooms. Everything was neat, clean, nicely arranged, and very old and worn. As they entered the larger bedroom, the newspapers pasted to the walls caught Lucile off guard. "Why the newspapers?" she asked.

"Insulation from the wind," Earl replied as he noticed the appalled expression on her face. He immediately added, "I am going to wallpaper over that."

Lucile asked, "Where is the lavatory?"

"It is out back," Earl said. "It is an outhouse."

The look on Lucile's face worsened before she said, "It is time to go."

"But you have not seen the two bedrooms upstairs."

Lucille said nothing more and started for the door. Earl pulled his old watch from his pocket and glanced at it. "We still have an hour before we must go."

"No, I need to go now," Lucile responded as she kept walking.

"All right," Earl said. He led Lucile back to the main room and blew out the lamps before walking her out to the buggy. After they were on their way again, Earl remarked, "Does not the air smell fresh?"

Lucile nodded, but said nothing. The ride was quiet, and soon Dolly had the buggy back in town.

"Leave me off at the church," Lucile said.

As directed, Earl stopped the rig at the church steps. He looked at Lucile and reached out for her hand, hoping for some sign that she might be pleased with something from the day. She pulled her hand away before he could touch her.

"Let me help you down," Earl said.

"No, I am fine," Lucile climbed from the buggy and started up the church steps. When she got to the top step, Earl called out, "Will I see you Thursday?"

Lucile stopped, looked back, and said, "I do not know." She turned and walked into the church.

Crushed by her response, Earl sat in the buggy for a time before he finally flipped the reins and said, "Let us go, Dolly." The horse instantly began pulling the buggy home. As Earl rode along, he looked up to the night sky. The twinkling stars shone down as he pondered on just how small man is, in respect to infinity. He rationalized the fact that his problems were tinier, in comparison. That realization helped him cope with the disheartening moments of the day.

Over the next week, Earl buried himself in his work. All three leases needed to be pumped and he needed to split more firewood. He had missed a lot of band practice, so he made sure to go to all of them. All the while, his mind reflected on how he could have avoided the traumatic events of Thanksgiving.

Earl toiled extra hard on Thursday, trying to forget Lucile. It seemed like whatever he did, it just was not good enough to win her affection. Though weary, when he got home, he stopped at his mailbox before going inside. As he pulled open the mailbox door, one letter stood out. He reached in and grabbed it. His eyes widened when he recognized the handwriting. Earl hastily opened the envelope and pulled a piece of paper from inside. Another paper fell to his feet as he unfolded the letter. The written words were short and to the point.

Dear Earl,

I must apologize for my actions when we last parted. It seems that, at times, life is not always as I picture it to be. I have one thing to ask of you. It is contained in the enclosed bulletin.

Yours truly,

Lucile

PS: Buy a new suit

Earl glanced around until he spied the piece of paper on the ground. He scooped it up and unfolded a write-up that confused him:

AUDITION

Auditions for pianist in the orchestra sponsored by the Odd Fellows Lodge will be held on Thursday, December 6. Anyone that is talented and is interested, please bring your credentials and come to the IOOF building at 6pm sharp. Be prepared to play at least two compositions of your choice.

Earl was confused. *Why would she send me this?* He knew all about the orchestra sponsored by the Odd Fellows Lodge. It was one of the finest orchestras in the area. It had launched the careers of some local musicians. But Earl had always felt that his piano skills were not strong enough. Obviously Lucile thought otherwise—or, in some fiendish way, did she want him to try and fail?

Earl took the letter and bulletin into his house, sat down on his rocker, and read them again. His mind raced through all the times he had tried to win Lucile's affection. All his efforts seemed to boil down to a few glorious moments and one stolen kiss. His mother's words kept ringing in his ears. *Perhaps Mama is right. Lucile would never be happy to live on a farm and be the wife of an oil worker. That may be why she continued to hold back, either because she does not care that much, or because she does not want to lower herself. Does her beauty transcend her true self?*

His mind thought on. *Should I return her letter? Should I go to the audition? The letter is so short that it seems almost heartless, like a forced farewell.* He wrestled with those thoughts until he fell asleep.

Earl jerked awake. It was dawn. He had slept in the rocker all night. He rushed to get to work, and finished by the early afternoon. As he saddled Dolly, he decided not to return a letter to Lucile. He rode to Pleasantville and boarded Dolly at the livery. He hopped the 3:00 PM trolley to Titusville and bought a new suit.

Thursday came. Earl was the first person to the audition. He handed his references to the three judges and sat down on a long wooden bench. Four more people came in behind him, handed in their paperwork, and sat down. The judges examined all the information given to them. One judge announced, "My name is John Olsen. This is Marcus Hamlin and Jacob Barberton. We welcome you to this audition. Now, when I call your name, please go to the piano and announce the title of the composition that you have chosen, and the composer's name. We will begin with Thomas Evermore."

Earl listened as each person was called to audition. All the while, he wondered why he had not been called first. He had gotten there ahead of the others. Three of the four contestants played religious church music, but then an older man played Beethoven extremely well. Earl thought to himself, *How can I win?*

Earl was finally the only one left on the bench. The judges began to whisper. It was obviously a debate. As one judge raised his voice, Earl overheard, "He is here. We will let him play." John Olsen immediately turned and looked at Earl. "You may proceed, Mr. Ames."

Earl immediately stood and walked over to the grand piano. He did not carry sheet music, as the others had. He never looked at the judges as he set down and focused on the keys. He spread his arms and lightly glided his fingers over the ivory, never causing a single note to sound. When his fingers reached the middle of the keyboard, he cleared his throat and announced, "'Reverie,' by Claude Debussy." The judges looked on in surprise as Earl began to play. At first his nervousness produced a choppy, mechanical sound. He closed his eyes, put his soul into the music, and played incessantly as notes flowed from the instrument.

Earl opened his eyes at the end of the composition and announced, "'Mazurka in A Minor, Opus 17, Number 4,' by Frédéric Chopin." He closed his eyes again and reached to his soul. The notes seemed flawless as tears ran down Earl's face, announcing that he was one with the music. When he finished, he tried to inconspicuously wipe his eyes. He looked at the panel of judges, but all he saw were astounded stares looking back. Finally, the gentleman in the middle stated, "I know who you are. You play trombone for the Pleasantville Band. I know where you live. I know who your parents are." He shook his head and asked, "Where did you learn to play like that?"

"My mama," Earl shyly said.

The man instantly replied, "Many people learn to play the piano from a relative, but you play with such emotion, you must have trained under someone."

"No," Earl responded. "I guess the way I play comes from within. I mean, I enjoy playing, so I practice a lot. That is, when I am not working or playing trombone."

The man looked to his colleagues before saying, "Because of your lack of references, we were debating whether to even let you audition, but an esteemed member asked us to let you." Olsen shook his head and said, "Who would have known?" He looked to his colleagues. "My mind is made up." The other two judges nodded their heads in agreement.

Mr. Olsen grabbed some papers and walked over to Earl. "Here is the music we are working on for our next presentation. We practice every Thursday at seven sharp."

"Yes sir," Earl replied. "And, thank you for this opportunity."

"You are welcome," Olsen replied, "but I feel the opportunity is ours."

CHAPTER 14
House Fire as the Government Seizes the Railroads

January 3, 1918

Earl awoke with the dawn. He reluctantly forged enough ambition to leave his warm bed and walk to the front room. He grabbed the poker and stoked the fire in the iron stove, then stepped to the iced-over window and scratched away the frost until he could peek out a small opening. The thermometer nailed to the porch post read ten below. It had now been below zero since the tenth of December. The roads were partly blocked by two feet of snow that had accumulated over those weeks.

Earl had worked tirelessly to thaw the lines and tanks at the oil leases, but the cold had hung on too long. Everything was frozen solid. There would be no oil pumping for a while.

He dressed and found something to eat just before a knock came at the door. He opened it to see his brother Arthur standing there, all bundled up, wearing snowshoes.

"Hello, Top. How are you on this brisk day?" Arthur spouted from behind the scarf he had pulled across his face.

"Fine, Artie. Come in, so I can close the door before all the warmth gets out."

Arthur stepped in and pulled his scarf down before continuing, "I am walking to Pleasantville to get the mail. Do you need anything?"

"Nothing I can think of."

"What are you doing today?" Arthur asked.

"After I do my chores, I think it is a good day to stay inside and practice music."

"Well, maybe we could hook Dolly to the sleigh and you could go with me."

Earl surmised out loud, "The only way two people could get down the roads today would be walking, horses, or a horse-drawn sleigh . . . yeah, we can do that, if you help with my chores first."

"I guess," Arthur grudgingly replied. "But, bundle up quickly so we can get going."

Soon the two had the chores done, the sleigh pulled out of the barn, and Dolly hooked to it. Earl paused to look across the field. Recurrent breezes were tossing the flurries about, crisscrossing them in the air before pausing, allowing the flakes to temporarily float toward the ground. The wind then swept up snowflakes and spun them, creating a snow devil. The conjured-up contrivance dashed across the field, desperately searching, before finding another place to hide in the white.

Yes, the snow is an obstacle to everyday life and, yes, it is cold. Winter displays a menacing beauty that demands respect from all living things.

Earl climbed onto the sleigh. He turned his face from the scathing wind before shouting, "Let us go, Dolly." He flicked the reins, and off they went.

After traveling a distance, the two came upon an extremely large drift blocking the road. Earl pulled back on the reins and the horse stopped. He examined the problem before commanding, "Dolly, we are going around." He flipped the reins and directed the horse off the road and into the field where the wind had swept away the snow to make the drift.

Once they passed the worst drifts, Earl pulled Dolly back onto the road. Just then, the sun peaked through the gray clouds, glorifying the winter wonderland. The flakes momentarily floated down as the wind paused.

This is the right moment, Arthur thought as he pulled his scarf down and said, "Top, I came to see you today for another reason." Arthur paused before blurting out, "I am going to enlist."

Earl's brow lifted before he spoke, through his scarf, "Does Mama know?"

"No. I was hoping you could be with me when I tell her."

"After all that happened on Thanksgiving, and then I did not come for Christmas, I am not sure my presence will be of help."

"I know it will," Arthur replied. "You are the eldest. Mama respects that, and will listen to you."

Arthur waited for a reply just as Earl glanced to the sky and spouted, "Look! That is a *lot* of smoke."

"Yes, it is. It looks to be coming from around Bugtown Road," Arthur replied.

"That is not far out of our way. Let us go see," Earl said, and Arthur agreed.

They traveled on to where trees bordered both sides of the road. The natural barrier blocked the wind, eliminating the drifts. Only a deep layer of powder lay in their way, making travel quicker.

When Earl turned Dolly onto the Bugtown Road, the smoke towered over them.

"It has to be the McDonald place!" Arthur bellowed as the flickering flames began to show through the barren trees.

"I am stopping Dolly here on the road," Earl said as he pulled back on the reins. "We cannot risk her spooking from the fire." Earl jumped from the sleigh and tied Dolly's reins to a sapling.

Arthur grabbed his snowshoes and quickly tied them on. He took off through the trees, towards the fire. Earl followed, but his brother could travel faster on snowshoes.

Arthur emerged from the woods to the shocking site of the Widow McDonald's house, completely engulfed in flames. He rushed over to the few dazed people who were standing nearby. Minutes later, Earl made it to the group and immediately wondered, *Why are they not fighting the fire?* Suddenly, the roof collapsed. Everyone quickly stepped back as Mr. Bauer, the next-door neighbor, cradled his arms around both Mrs. McDonald and her aunt, Mary Sedoris, who lived with her. Both women screamed out in grief-stricken agony.

Earl looked around and then asked, "Where is Sarah?" She was McDonald's invalid daughter. Earl knew her well. He had gone to school with Sarah, until a bout with diphtheria took her mind.

William Enos, a border, living at the McDonald house, said nothing as he slightly shook his head. It was obvious that Sarah, being bedridden, had not made it out.

The heat caused everyone to take another step back just as the inferno brought the sidewalls to the ground. The crackling fire roared as the flames shot higher into the sky, hastily consuming what was left of the house into just a pile of burning rubble.

With tears brimming in his eyes, William looked at the Ames brothers and said, "The fire started upstairs, I do not know why, probably from the chimney. We were in the kitchen. Mrs. McDonald was making breakfast when I heard a crackling sound. I went over and opened the door to the upstairs; all I saw was the second floor completely ablaze. Mrs. McDonald was right behind me. She screamed and tried to rush up the steps to save Sarah, but it was hopeless. Fire was completely blocking the way. The flames were growing so fast, I knew I only had moments to grab her and Mary and pull them outside before the ceiling would cave in. I then ran to the barn and got buckets, but when I tried the outside water pump, it was frozen solid." He stopped momentarily, trying to calm his emotions. Then, with pain in his voice, he said, "I heard no cries for help and I heard no screaming. I pray to God that the smoke got Sarah before the flames."

He stopped again, and continued, "Mr. Bauer told his son to take the horse and ride to Titusville to get the fire department, but that was futile. The roads are almost impassible, and it was already too late. I stopped the boy just before he left and told him to inform the authorities and the coroner." William quit talking and stood in a daze. He finally said, "I will hold up in the barn until the coroner gets here—which, with this weather, may take some time." He walked away.

Earl and Arthur stood alone; their hearts heavy with sorrow. The hellish echo of the fire's snapping and cracking was shouting that it would burn everything to ashes before any attempt could be made to recover Sarah's remains. (This event was reported by the Titusville Herald Newspaper, January 3, 1918.)

Without a word, Arthur turned and walked back to the sleigh. Earl followed. The tragedy left only silence and a lump in each of their throats as they rode on into town.

Constantly heating houses with wood-fired stoves and open-hearth fireplaces during a long cold spell created buildup of creosote in chimneys. At times, this allowed fires to start. Charles Kelly had lost his house a few weeks earlier, but everyone got out alive, there.

Arthur finally spoke. "Top, I feel terrible about Sarah. This life was so cruel to her."

"I know, Artie," Earl replied. "I feel terrible, too. Sarah was a wonderful soul who already suffered so much, with the loss of her father. Then disease took her mind, and now this. There must be a special place in heaven for her."

The silence resumed until Arthur said, "Let us stop by the parsonage and tell Reverend Barber. He will comfort the family and notify those who can donate to help them. I know Mama and Father will. I will, too."

"Yes, me too," Earl replied.

After the stop at the parsonage, the quiet journey continued to the post office. When Earl stopped Dolly, Arthur jumped from the sleigh and went inside. Soon he came back out with a bundle of letters and six days of newspapers. Arthur tossed the mail onto the sleigh seat and climbed back aboard. Earl flipped the reins and Dolly started for home.

They rode back through the winter wonderland until reaching Earl's house again. After Dolly was unhooked and put in the barn, the two brothers went inside.

Arthur immediately went to the stove and warmed his frozen hands. Earl did the same.

The shock of Sarah's death was still rambling through their minds when Arthur stepped away and sat down at the table. He untied the bundle of mail and began sorting it as Earl joined him. "Here," Arthur said as he handed Earl a letter.

Earl looked intensely at the envelope before opening it. Arthur sat patiently, he had seen who the letter was from and was now waiting for a response. Earl pulled the paperwork from inside the envelope and shuffled through it, but still no explanation. Arthur finally grabbed one of December's newspapers and began to read. "*What?*" he cried out. "The government is taking over the railroads!"

Earl looked up from his letter and asked, "Why?"

Arthur paraphrased, "It says that President Wilson has proclaimed that the railroads are being taken over under authority granted to Congress through the Secretary of War. Wilson states here that the war is as much about manpower as it is about supplies, and the transportation system of this country must be organized to ship resources to the front faster." Arthur read the next few words exactly as written. "This seizure will eliminate inessential travel."

"We are already dealing with shortages because the government commandeered the ships," Earl complained. "Now they are seizing the railroads so we cannot travel on them freely?"

"I know," Arthur responded. "It seems these sacrifices for the war are growing more all the time." (Reported by the Associated Press via the Titusville Hearld Newspaper, December 29, 1917, Page 1.)

"Yes," Earl replied as his attention turned back to the letter in his hand.

"Well?" Arthur asked.

"Well, what?" Earl responded.

"Who is the letter from?" Arthur asked in an annoyed voice, although he already knew.

"It is my questionnaire for the conscription," Earl responded, "It appears that I am going to be drafted. I thought that maybe I would get through the war without that happening."

"Well, if I get one of those letters, it will solve my issue," Arthur replied. "But if you take the draft, you are going to be put where they want. At least if you enlist, you can choose what branch you want to serve in." Arthur shifted the conversation. "Albo received another letter from Jack Litzinger a few weeks ago. It was addressed to all of us. Jack wrote that he finished basic training and was shipping out to France. That is pretty much all he said, other than that he wanted to know if any of us had enlisted or been drafted."

"Jack must be homesick already," Earl said.

"I do not think so," Arthur replied, "but maybe he misses us. He has been around for so long; he thinks he is a brother."

"You are right."

Arthur changed the subject. "Well, I must go." He stepped over to his snowshoes and tied them on before putting on his coat and gloves. He flipped up his hood and grabbed the bundle of mail as he said, "I am telling Father and Mama on Tuesday evening. I hope you will be there." Arthur pulled his scarf over his face. He turned and waved goodbye before going out the door.

Earl noticed the self-assurance in Arthur's voice as he left. Earl also knew how steadfast his mother could be. With the family tension surrounding him, Earl felt it might only hinder Arthur if he showed up. His mind reflected on Sarah, again. Empathy filled his soul as he wrestled with the thought of what else he could have done … but there was nothing. He looked back to the missive. He filled in the answers and put the envelope in his mailbox the next morning. *With the way the weather is, it may sit in the box for a week,* he thought. *That is all right by me.*

CHAPTER 15
Backfire and Job Loss

February and March 1918

February started out colder than January had. On Monday the fourth, the mercury dropped to 18 below zero, and on Tuesday, it went to 30 below. The weather dominated almost everything.

However, during the next two weeks a warming trend began. The temperature reached above freezing for the first time since early December. Rain began to fall, causing the snow to melt faster. The ice barricading the creeks and riverbeds caused the water to find alternative avenues to rush away.

Pine Creek was one of the waterways that had already escaped its banks, flooding every low-lying area close by. The floating ice plowed down everything in its way, including two of the wells of the Enterprise lease. As Dolly and Earl stood on dry ground, they looked out at the well jacks protruding from the water. Earl needed to get a closer look, but the path to those wells was also underwater. He forged a makeshift walkway through the dense, dead goldenrod, and the blackberry and burr bushes that had built a fortress around the location.

Like sentries, the vegetation fought his every step, snagging his coveralls, pulling at his coat, and leaving burrs on his clothing, seemingly trying to block his way. He crushed their resistance until he had gone far enough to see. The jerk lines and pipes were broken and twisted in the ice. He shook his head and muttered, "The power of nature is amazing. This will take time to repair. Maybe I can get Mr. Piffer to hire Artie to help me. But nothing is going to get done until this water recedes." He forged his way back through the trail he had created and went about unhooking the lines and closing off the valves that led to those two wells.

His quest to start the rest of the lease led Earl and Dolly back to the powerhouse. Earl spent the rest of the morning thawing the outside water lines by pouring crude oil over them and lighting them off. He gathered every kerosene lantern available—even the two old Yellow Dog lanterns that burned crude oil. He strategically placed those lanterns under and against the engine and lit them. Hopefully, their warmth would eventually be enough that he could start the engine. The heating would take time, but he needed to follow the lines to make sure they and the other wells were undamaged anyway. He mounted Dolly, and they rode the lease.

In late afternoon, Earl rode Dolly back to the powerhouse. He tied her to the hitching post outside and entered the building, stepped over to the engine, and touched it. The metal felt warm. The lanterns may have done their job. He turned a small petcock valve, and water trickled out. It had thawed enough. He turned on the field gas and lit the hot tube before pulling the lanterns away and filling the oilers.

With all his preparation, it was still a struggle to roll the flywheel back on an engine that had sat idle so long in subzero weather. With all his might, he forced the wheel back and forth to suck fuel into the cylinder. He finally got the wheel back enough to charge the main cylinder. He then pushed the wheel forward, but it moved too slowly to start. He repeated the process again and again. Frustrated, he adjusted the sector valve and then yanked the wheel forward with all his might, simultaneously placing his whole foot on the spoke and allowing his full body weight to slam down on the flywheel.

BANG! Backfire! The wheel violently jerked. Dolly reared outside from the sudden noise, while, in the building, Earl flew into the air. He hit the floor so hard that he saw white. He gasped to regain the breath that had been knocked from his lungs. Excruciating pain stabbed his body. As he laid there moaning, his father's words reflected in his mind. *Son, Reid engines can backfire. If, for some reason, you must use your foot on the spoke of the flywheel to start one, be careful! A backfire can throw you and break your leg, or worse. Make sure you just place the toe of your boot on the spoke. That way, it may just slip off, if a backfire would occur.*

His father's words continued echoing in his mind as he slightly moved his leg. The pain escalated at his knee. He had no choice—no one was coming to help, so he had to get up. He cried out in agony while struggling to his feet. After standing a moment to let the pain ease some, he torturously took one step, and then another. He reached the valves and turned them off. He then slowly limped outside to Dolly and untied her reins before painfully pulling himself up onto the saddle. He hunched forward and hugged Dolly's neck while muttering, "Let us go, girl." The horse took him home.

After a week, Earl was hobbling around better, using his grandfather's cane. No matter how much it hurt, he had chores to do, band practice, and two oil leases to operate.

He was thankful that Albert and Arthur had come over the day before and then gone with him to start the Enterprise lease.

However, through those days, the cold had returned. The roads were now just frozen deep ruts and iced-over mud puddles, making travel difficult.

Earl was in the barn doing chores when he heard a motor running outside. He grabbed his cane before opening the barn door. He saw his father and mother sitting in Uncle John's model T. The moment Almon saw Earl, he got out and walked over while Ella waved from the auto.

"Hello, Father."

"Hello, Top. I am so glad to see you standing. From what your brothers told us this morning, I expected you to be inside, lying down."

"No, I still have work to do."

"I understand," Almon said before asking, "but, tell me truthfully: how do you feel?"

"I am fine," Earl replied.

"Well, seeing the way you lean on that cane, I do not know if I believe that." Almon put on his fatherly voice and said, "Son, I know you and your brothers were young when I taught you how to run a lease. Did you not remember my warning about Reid engines?"

"Yes. . . I remembered it all, just as I landed on the floor."

Almon smiled and replied, "You do not know how thankful your mother and I are that you did not get hurt worse."

Earl changed the subject. "What brings you and Mama out here today?"

"To check on you . . . and to have you patch things up with her. She cried all Christmas Day when you did not show up."

Earl said nothing as he hobbled, with his cane, towards the automobile. Almon followed as Ella immediately climbed out and ran to embrace Earl.

"I am so sorry, Top."

"It is all right Mama. I am sorry, too."

After a long embrace, Ella pulled away and said, "Now, let me see your leg."

"No, it is fine."

"It cannot be fine when I see you hobbling with your grandfather's cane." Ella changed the subject. "I made some chicken noodle soup for you. It will help you heal." She turned and rushed back to the car to retrieve a large, covered bowl, then carried it back to where Earl and Almon were standing. "Here," she said to Almon. "Take this inside for your son. It is already cold because it took us so long to get here."

"It was your idea to use John's autocar," Almon replied in a disturbed tone. "If we had just taken Prince and the buggy, we would have been here much earlier."

"Why is that?" Earl asked inquisitively.

"Because of the ruts in the roads." Almon pointed to the vehicle. "They are hub-deep, in places. The axles bottom out, and then we are stuck. The buggy is higher off the ground. Prince would have just stepped around those ruts."

"How did you two get here, then?" Earl asked.

"Well, I did what most people who own an auto-car in this area do. I had your mother drive while I walked ahead with an axe and chopped down the deepest ruts."

"I told you to drive off to the side of those ruts," Ella ranted.

Almon shot back, "There was not enough room! We would have slipped into a gulley and that contraption would have just sat there until we could get a team of horses to pull it out!"

Earl immediately changed the subject, hoping to cool the situation. "It is cold out here. Let us go inside and have some of this soup."

Ella and Almon both looked at Earl. Almon shrugged and they all walked to the house. The two men sat down and talked as Ella warmed up the soup. She finally brought the steaming pot to the table and set it down. She looked at Almon and said, "Are you going to tell him?"

Almon looked at Ella before turning back to Earl. "Your Uncle Romey got his draft notice. He caught the train to Warren today, to take his physical."

Ella's eyes welled up as she said in a demanding voice, "Tell him the other news."

Earl looked back to Almon, who lowered his head and meekly said, "I am losing my job. Carlen sold out to Universal Drilling, and I am not being taken on." Almon staunchly added, "They told me that they already have too many employees that can do what I do. I told them they will never find anyone that can do that job as well as me!"

Ella, now with tears running down her cheeks, finished the story. "Universal will not let us stay in our house. We even offered to pay more rent, but they said they need it for an employee."

Almon added, "The house has always been company-owned. Now it belongs to Universal."

Ella hesitated before stating, "I do not know what we are going to do." She walked over to the window and stood with her back to the men.

Earl heard his mother's sniffling. It was too much. Instantly, he spoke out, "You can live here."

"No, that is not why we came to see you," Almon replied. "Besides, it is too small for the whole family, and Carlen told me that he has a job for me on his brother's lease."

With her back still turned, Ella blurted out, "But that job is miles away in Ohio, and it does not pay near enough."

"Ella. . ." Almon pleaded.

Earl immediately spoke up. "You two need to know that I received my questionnaire. I filled it out and mailed it . . . I had to." Ella turned from the window to look at Earl as he continued, "The notice to take my physical will come next. So, this little place will not be crowded, with Artie and me gone."

"*What*!" Ella and Almon cried in unison. "Where is Artie going?"

Earl instantly clammed up. Obviously, Arthur had not told them.

"Did he enlist?" Ella blurted out. She looked intensely at Earl while exclaiming, "Son, you have that same look on your face that you did when you were small. It tattles on you. What are you not saying?"

"Ahhh..." Earl stalled as he faced the dilemma. He finally narrated his conjured-up story. "When he told me, he had not enlisted yet, but I guess he then did."

"It is that Rolands girl!" Ella surmised. "He has always been sweet on her. She is nothing but a scurry-wisher." (Slang for someone who wishfully desires one thing one moment, then something different in the next moment.) "She probably talked him into enlisting!"

"No," Earl responded, "you know Artie is not that shallow. He feels it is his duty to enlist."

Ella began rambling. "I have told you boys over and over not to go. Both your grandfathers came back from the Civil War as hollow men. What did not wound their bodies wounded their souls."

"Ella," Almon coaxed, "Earl does not have a choice, and he is right about Artie."

Ella blandly replied, "Almon, we are losing everything—your job, our home and now my brother—and our sons are leaving."

"Dear, this is breaking my heart also," Almon replied. "These are hard times for everyone—but as far as a job, I will find one and we will find another place to live."

Ella never replied as she grabbed her coat and walked outside.

Almon looked back to Earl and said, "I must take her home."

"I understand, Father, but please consider my offer. It will help me by not letting this place sit vacant while I am gone."

"I will talk to her," Almon replied just before he hugged his son and left.

That evening, Earl strapped his trombone and cane onto Dolly and rode to band practice. It was a slow ride, but the last thing he needed was for Dolly to go lame from stumbling on the rutted road.

After practice, Lewis Watson, the band leader, approached Earl. "Hello, it's good to see you here tonight, Earl. I have to say that I could not help but notice your limping."

"I got hurt on the lease," Earl replied, "but I am healing."

"That is good," Lewis replied, before saying, "I must ask something else. I heard that you were accepted to play piano with that orchestra sponsored by the IOOF. You are not leaving us, are you?"

"No, I can do both. Besides, I have done nothing with that orchestra, yet. They canceled everything because of that 'Fuelless Monday' legislation that started in January."

Lewis replied, "I can understand the 'Food Will Win The War' campaign, with its "Meatless Mondays" and "Wheatless Wednesdays." But how shutting down commerce on Mondays to conserve coal is helping, I cannot understand. But, I did hear they are going to end that program soon."

Lewis reverted to what he wanted to say. "Anyway, I know no one else that can expertly play both the piano and trombone. Which brings me to the proposition I have for you. I was approached by the Red Cross about having you accompany a pianist at a Thrift Stamp Entertainment event."

"Why me?"

"They asked for our best trombone player."

Earl timidly accepted the compliment before asking, "Who is the pianist?"

"I do not know. Probably someone from the Red Cross."

Earl asked, "What is a Thrift Stamp Entertainment event, anyway?"

"Thrift Stamps are a new program the government started that makes it easier for people to invest in the war effort. Now, different organizations have been having social events to bring people in for entertainment in the hope they will buy the new stamps. Twenty-five-cents gets you one. After you collect sixteen, it earns you one savings stamp. Collect twenty savings stamps and you get a savings certificate. It is an easier way to earn some interest while helping our government."

Mr. Watson handed Earl a sheet of paper. "Here is the list of songs for the event. You know them all—we play them all the time —so there is no need for practice. It takes place two Fridays from now. Be at the Red Cross building by seven."

"All right," Earl replied while realizing that, instead of volunteering, he had just been drafted.

"Take care of yourself," Mr. Watson said just before he walked away.

Earl glanced at the song list and then grabbed his trombone case and cane and limped out the door. Instantly, he noticed Arthur standing by Dolly. Earl walked over, looking for any expression on Arthur's face.

"How is the knee feeling, Top?" was the first thing Arthur said.

"It is getting better," Earl responded as he braced himself for the verbal confrontation he felt was coming. He began strapping his horn case onto Dolly as his mind reckoned that he should fire the first shot. "I am sorry, Artie, but you told me that you were telling Mama and Father over a week ago."

"Do not be sorry, Top. You handled it just like I knew you would. They were downhearted, but neither of them laid into me."

"I am glad of that," Earl responded with a sigh. "So, why did you not come into practice?"

"Because I am leaving in a few days. I quit school today and was waiting for Mr. Watson to come out so I can tell him. I did not want to do that in front of everyone."

"Well, what branch did you choose?"

"The cavalry, just like both our Granddads," Arthur proudly replied.

Earl asked, "Where is Albo? I expected him to be here tonight, also."

"He got on at Universal Drilling as a tool dresser. They got way behind during that cold spell, so he is working some long hours."

"Albo took a job with the company that just let our father go?"

"Father losing his job is why Albo went to work for them. He tried to get their home back by becoming an employee. But Universal had already rented it to some other worker. Father told him to stay on anyway, seeing as the pay is higher than any other company around these parts. Albo said that he can help the family better, now."

"I told them to come live at my place," Earl interjected.

"I know," Arthur responded.

Just then, Mr. Watson came walking out the door. Knowing that it might be a long time before they saw each other again, Earl reached out his hand to shake. Instead, Arthur grabbed him in a manly hug and said, in a quivering voice, "I am going to miss you, Top."

"Me too, Artie, me too," Earl replied.

"I have to go," Arthur said as he broke their embrace and started towards Watson.

"Write!" Earl bellowed out.

Arthur turned and shouted back, "I will!"

CHAPTER 16
Thrift Stamps and Eviction

April 12, 1918

I t was Friday. Earl had worked all day, finishing the rebuilding of
the two wells that had been destroyed in February. He kept an
eye on the time until he had to leave for the Thrift Stamp show. He
rode Dolly home, cleaned up, and changed his clothes. He lashed his
trombone case to Dolly's saddle before glancing at his old watch.
"There is plenty of time," he said to Dolly as he mounted the horse
and flicked the reins. They headed for town.

Upon arriving, Earl tied Dolly to the hitching post out front. He
pulled the usual carrot from his pocket. Dolly grabbed it from his
hand with her teeth and began munching. He patted her neck and
then untethered his trombone from the saddle. He climbed the steps
to the front door of the church and opened it. A woman with a Red
Cross pin on her blouse met him. She looked at the case in his hand
and said, in an irritated voice, "You must be the trombone player.
Where have you been? The show is about to start. You were
supposed to be here over two hours ago, to practice with the
pianist!"

"I was told to be here by seven," Earl replied in a defensive tone.

"Well, I hope she and you are good enough to pull this off
without embarrassing our chapter." The woman commanded,
"Follow me!" She led Earl to a room off the side of the pulpit. "You
can put your case in here," she said, "and then wait until I come get
you. What is your name, so that I can tell the announcer?"

"Earl Ames."

The woman left. Earl knelt and was pulling his trombone from its case when he heard muffled applause through the walls. A man's voice addressed the crowd with a long patriotic speech sprinkled with the pitch to buy thrift stamps.

Finally, Earl heard the introduction of a minstrel show. Someone began to accompany the sketch on a piano. His curiosity got the best of him. He stepped from the room over to the edge of the stage curtain. Standing to the side of the pulpit area, he could see the puppeteers hiding behind their fabricated structure, creating a show with just figurines made mostly of cloth and wood. The crowd intermittingly laughed as the puppets acted out their antics. Earl laughed also. He peeked around the curtain to scan the crowd. *There!* He saw an older woman playing the piano that was in front of the crowded pews. *That must be who I am playing with,* he surmised. He walked back to the room.

As Earl sat waiting, he again heard the muffled voice introduce another act, then another, and then another. Finally, the woman reappeared at the door and said, "I did not expect you to stay in this room the whole time. I just meant for you to be close by so that I could find you ... well, follow me."

Earl stood as he wondered, *Did she really mean that? Or does she think she punished me for being late?* With his trombone in hand, he followed the woman as they walked out a side door and around to the front of the church. As they walked in, she began instructing. "You are on next." She pointed while continuing, "We will stand at that door that leads into the nave. When I open it, you walk straight down the aisle to the piano. The pianist will be walking down the other aisle, in unison with you."

Earl nodded nervously just as they reached the door. The wait seemed long until the narrator paused from his pitch. "You are on," the woman said as she flung the door open. Earl began walking. He had only gone a short distance before glancing over to the other aisle.

"*What!*?" he exclaimed, just as the announcer spoke. "For our last performance of the night, we have Miss Lucile Lake on the piano, accompanied by Mr. Earl Ames of the Pleasantville Band on his trombone. They will perform some well-known songs for your listening pleasure."

The crowd applauded as Lucile and Earl walked on. The two reached the piano at the same time. Lucile sat down at the bench, flashed her eyes up at Earl, and said, "We start with 'My Country Tis of Thee.' I will lead off. Try to stay in tempo."

Earl, still perplexed, nodded and raised his trombone to his lips, trying to hide behind it in fear of what notes might come from Lucile's playing. The two began. The harmony of their music seemed to say that they had played together for years.

The final song was 'America the Beautiful.' The crowd broke out in song with the first few notes. When the song ended, loud cheering and more applause filled the auditorium. The narrator was still pitching thrift stamps as Earl smiled at the crowd, while commenting from the side of his mouth, "You played superbly."

Lucile stood from the piano and curtsied while replying, "I know. I have been practicing for weeks."

"I did not know I would be accompanying you," Earl injected.

"Nor did I," Lucile replied, "but if you had been on time, we both would have known."

"That was not my fault," Earl rebutted, "but still, I just cannot believe . . ."

Lucile interrupted him mid-sentence, saying, "I must confess that my father made a large donation with the stipulation that I play piano in the show."

"Oh," was all Earl could say.

Everything got awkward from there. Earl stood gazing at Lucile as she gazed back. The crowd noise filled the air as emotion filled Earl, and he suddenly blurted out, "May I call on you?"

Lucile's eyes opened wide before she uttered, "Yes."

The two stood a moment longer before Lucile said, "I must go."

"When may I call?" Earl forwardly asked, not wanting her to leave without a date.

"Send me a letter first," she replied just before she walked away.

What? A letter? Earl was still confused as he slightly waved goodbye. *Is this chance meeting destiny? Or a degree of disharmony?*

Earl spent the next few days at work grappling with his mind, trying to find the words to write Lucile and at the same time trying to understand what did not seem logical. He made his way home that evening to find his father standing on his porch.

"Hello, Top," Almon said as Earl got close.

"Hello, Father. Have you been waiting long?"

"Not at all. Prince and I just got here a little while ago." Almon noted, "I see you have already done away with the cane."

"Yes. I still limp a little, but I am good enough to go without it, now."

Earl opened the door and the two men stepped inside. Almon sat down at the table as Earl lit a couple of lamps while asking, "So, Father, what brings you here tonight?"

"I wanted to tell you that I took that job in Ohio. Your mother is right. It does not pay enough, but I have asked around, and no one seems to be hiring right now. I guess at times, a man has no choice but to take what is offered."

"I understand," Earl replied as he sat down.

Almon continued, "I will be gone for two weeks at a time. My new boss said I can stay in their bunkhouse shanty, but I need to take you up on your offer. Mother, Albo, Russell, and Clara need a place to live until I can find other arrangements."

"That is fine," Earl replied. "Everyone can stay as long as they like."

"We need to move quickly, though," Almon responded. "I need to be in Ohio in three days."

"Fine," Earl said. "We can store in the barn what you do not need in the house."

"Thank you, son." Almon continued, in a defeated tone, "I need to get home now, to start loading the household."

"I will come to help," Earl replied.

"No," Almon stated as he stood, "you have already done enough, and your mother and I need some time alone. The humility of this night will bring us to tears."

"All right," Earl said as he stood. He patted Almon on the back as they walked to the door. Almon then turned and hugged his son before walking out.

Dawn found Earl working the Jameson lease. It was vital that he run the oil today, yet he had to get home to help the family move. He rushed, and by early afternoon had finished. He rode Dolly back to his house, unsaddled her, and hooked her to his wagon. That is when he heard it—a faint sound on the wind. Curious, he walked to the front of his house and looked down the freshly dragged road. The sun's rays contrasted the tracts of the dogwoods as their vivid white splashed among the budding trees along the berm. The intermittent tones seemed to emanate off them and the rest of the woods. Then he recognized it. They were piano notes—but what song was being played?

He listened intently before saying out loud, "'Maple Leaf Rag,' by Scott Joplin." It was a lively tune that he knew well, and it was getting louder. He squinted to see a wagon coming from far off. As the rig drew closer, he recognized Prince pulling it. Almon and Albert were sitting on the wagon seat with little Clara sitting between them.

Russell, along with Shep, must be sitting on the top of the old upright piano in the back of the wagon, Earl surmised. *And Mama will be the one pounding on the keys.* The music, along with the noises of a moving wagon, continued as Almon finally pulled the rig into the drive. Everyone waved as they passed by Earl and stopped at the barn.

Earl walked over as everyone climbed off, except for Shep and Ella. She continued playing to the end of the song. She then looked at Earl and said, "Top, I felt that song might bring back memories for you."

"It did, Mama, it did."

"It is time to get off, Shep," Ella said as the dog jumped down. She addressed the piano. "And you must rest in the barn." She stood up from the bench to climb down.

"No, Mama," Earl called out. "This piano belongs in the house. It is family."

"But there is not enough room," Almon spoke up.

"We will make room. No matter what."

CHAPTER 17
The Storm and the Letter

May 20, 1918

Another day found Earl at the Enterprise powerhouse, sewing a rip in the wide leather belt that ran from the engine to the eccentric gear. He was deep in thought as he toiled, grappling over what to write to Lucile. It had already been too long. His letter could be rejected for that reason alone. With that in mind, he stopped working and sat down on an old chair leaning against the wall. He pulled paper and a pencil from his pocket and began writing, then scribbling, then writing again. Deep in thought, he never noticed the far-off rumble of thunder. He never noticed the wind pick up as it creaked the old powerhouse walls.

Suddenly, a loud crack from a lightning strike startled him. Earl jumped from the chair, tossing his paper and pencil just as ensuing thunder vibrated the building. He heard Dolly give out a high-pitched neigh. He ran outside to find the horse rearing and jerking back on her tied-up reins. He pulled off his coat and threw it over Dolly's eyes, then unleashed her from the hitch post just as the wind began to rage—rain began pelting them. Crack! Lightning flashed again as deafening thunder roared. Earl held tightly to the reins as Dolly continued to jitter about.

"It is all right, Dolly. It is all right, girl," he repeated, until the horse settled enough that he could pull her into the powerhouse. He tied the reins to a pipe and put his hand to Dolly's neck to pet her while he continued talking in a calm manner. A sudden burst of wind slammed the door shut and yanked at the corrugated steel panels of the building—the horse jerked again. A cloudburst began hammering on the steel roof, causing a deafening noise. Lightning flashed as the thunder cracked again and again. Earl glanced back and forth, nervously wondering if the powerhouse might collapse or be blown apart.

The torrent then ended as abruptly as it started. A sudden peacefulness overtook the air, along with the sound of rainwater draining off the roof. Earl pulled his coat from Dolly's eyes and turned her around. He pushed the door open and led her outside to a sunny day with clear blue skies. A concert of raindrops still dripping from the trees tapped out that the bad weather had passed. Earl looked east. The sky was black with the storm clouds that had just passed over. Someone else would now experience nature's fury.

He tied Dolly to the hitching post before going back inside to retrieve his things. He picked up his coat and pulled it on before walking back to the chair. He looked down. There his paper lay, in a puddle of water on the oil-crusted dirt floor. He grabbed his pencil before trying to pick up the waterlogged paper. The few words he had meticulously composed were now faded lines on bits of paper that tore apart at the touch of his hand. He shook his head as he wadded the paper pieces into a ball and threw it. He walked back out to Dolly and climbed onto her saddle. "Let us go girl. We have to follow the lines and check the well jacks for damage."

Between the storm and the loss of his words to Lucile, Earl gave up the day after inspecting the lease. He rode Dolly home, unsaddled the horse, and put her in the corral.

When he went to the house and opened the door, the wonderful smell of home cooking filled the air. Ella and little Clara both turned from the stove as Ella said, "You are home early. Dinner is not quite ready yet."

"Yes," Clara said as she pointed her finger at Earl.

Earl smiled and replied, "That is fine. I have work to do in the barn."

Just then, Russell came running in with a handful of mail. He excitedly exclaimed, "I just talked to Mr. Woods, the mailman. He said that lightning from the storm hit one of those big holding tanks at the Tidewater Pump Station." (Reported in the Titusville Hearld

Newspaper, May 21, 1918, Page 5.)

"He said it blew up. There is fire and smoke everywhere. Can we go see?"

"No, Russell," Earl responded. "I have things to do, yet, before dark."

"But, Top," Russell pleaded, "Mr. Woods said there is a giant crowd watching. You will probably know some people there."

"No, Russell," Earl repeated. "Besides, you have chores to do."

Discouraged, Russell huffed and left. Earl went out to the barn and climbed up into the hay loft. He retrieved a tablet that he had stuffed in the rafters the last time he had written there, then sat down on a hay bale and pulled the pencil from his pocket. His mind stumbled again, until finally the words began to flow.

> My dearest Lucile,
>
> I have wrestled for days over what to write to you. I must admit that I had previously given up—and then I saw you again. I know your world is different from mine, leaving me nothing to offer other than words of what I see, what I know, and what I feel.
>
> As the raindrops fall, they rush to the streams. And, from the moment we met, you filled my mind like streams fill the rivers. Yet, it is more than your beauty. You unlock, in me, a place beyond the heart.
>
> When you walk by, I follow your every move. My hope is that you glance my way with those eyes that flash like the lightning of a summer storm, yet reveal the promise of a blue sky, tomorrow.
>
> The fields of wheat gently wave like your flaxen hair in the breeze and your voice whispers to me on the wind.
>
> This vision I hold has led me to the edge of a dream. If I step in . . . are you there?
>
> Earl

He mailed the letter the next morning. Four days afterward, Dolly and Earl were harrowing one of the fields. It was a beautiful spring day. The sun was high in a sky of crystal blue.

"Whoa, girl," Earl commanded. Dolly stopped and began flicking her tail. She snorted, almost as if annoyed. "I know, girl; I know. We will be moving on in a moment." Earl reached down and pulled sod from the harrows. He stood and wiped the sweat from his brow when he noticed a dust cloud. It was far off, but had to be from a moving vehicle that was following the dirt road that zigzagged along the fence rows. He watched until an automobile came into view. The flashy vehicle appeared to be traveling faster than it should. It slowed and stopped at the edge of his field. After a moment, the driver's door opened and a woman climbed out. She began walking his way. As she drew closer, Earl recognized her.

He stood by Dolly as she approached. She stopped a few feet away and said, "I stopped by your house. I figured you would be working, so I was going to leave a note on your door. I was surprised to find your family there. I knew that leaving a note was not going to work. Then Russell told me where you were." Lucile said nothing more as she stood, staring at Earl. Her eyes seemed to be saying what he had hoped to hear. He finally took a step forward and she lunged into his arms. They embraced and kissed. After a time, she pulled back and asked, "How do you do the things you do? How do you write such things? How do you play music so beautifully?"

Earl never answered. He finally asked, "What was written in your note?"

"One word," Lucile responded. She noticed the puzzled look on Earl's face and said, "The answer to your question."

CHAPTER 18
War Outside of Chateau Thierry

Early July 1918

J ack Litzinger had been in training since his first day of enlistment. The 23-year-old had always shown a fearless determination. That attribute, along with the government's call to arms, had led him to join the army.

He, along with his fellow soldiers, boarded a troop carrier ship and journeyed eight days to France with the American Expeditionary Forces. After arriving, his battalion was held in reserve for more training. 'It seems as though I will never get into the fight,' Jack wrote in his letter addressed to Albo Ames and his brothers Artie and Top.

Then the afternoon came when the Sergeant gathered everyone in the platoon. "All right, boys," he said, "get your gear. Lieutenant says we march at sixteen hundred hours."

One of the recruits shouted out, "Where are we going, Sarge?"

"Some place called Chateau Thierry."

Anxiousness filled the troops as they hurriedly packed their backpacks and haversacks. With guns shouldered, they lined up with the rest of the brigade and marched a few miles to the railroad depot. Once there, they gathered on a platform before cramming into a group of open rail cars. "Move over, Jack," said Percy Long.

A slender, sandy-haired man of thirty, Percy was the ammunition carrier and the other member of the two-man machine rifle team. Being older, and having a family back home, Percy was more conscientious than a lot of soldiers.

Jack made room for Percy just as the train unlocked its brakes with a hiss. A clang sounded out with each car when its hitch slack came taut. The train began to move slowly, at first, until the locomotive chugged up to speed. The journey had begun.

The breeze caused by its movement felt good on such a beautiful July afternoon. As they traveled through the French countryside, Jack noticed a silhouette on the horizon. A hill with a flat top at the beginning of a mountainous area. 'Looks like Goodwill Hill,' he muttered.

"Goodwill Hill?" Percy asked.

Not expecting to be overheard, Jack never looked at Percy as he explained, "A place back home that I know well."

"Maybe all of this reminds you of home, Jack," Percy remarked, "but I grew up in Brooklyn. The only thing that reminds me of home is the noise and occasional whiff of coal smoke from this train. I do have to admit, though: a day like this makes it hard to believe there is a war going on out there."

"I know."

The journey continued as afternoon turned to evening. It was some time after dark when the locomotive switched off its headlight and slowed, leaving some soldiers uneasy while others laughed and joked. The train traveled on with only moonlight to show the way. Soon, the chugging slowed further until the train came to a stop at a makeshift platform. The Sergeant must have been the first one whose feet hit the ground. He appeared in the moonlight, walking briskly along the side of the cars, shouting, "Unload! unload! You can rest over there." He pointed toward a few trees silhouetting the night sky and continued, "no fires! Smith, Walker, Jones, and Fields, you have first watch!" He moved to the next car and repeated the command. Other officers down the line were giving similar orders.

Jack and Percy unloaded and walked to the trees. Just on the other side was a shallow trench that stretched for what appeared to be hundreds of yards. Located at a higher elevation than the surrounding terrain, the moonlit view from that position went on for miles to the outline of some distant mountains.

Percy looked at what was nothing more than a wide ditch and remarked, "at least we did not have to dig it."

A long line of troops noisily climbed in. Soon, the night's silence was broken only by someone's furtive muttering, the sound of crickets, and the far-off rumble of shelling.

As they lay against the side of the ditch, Jack glanced north. A distant glow momentarily flashed in the sky before each remote boom. "I wonder what it is like to be there tonight?" Jack commented.

Percy opened his eyes and replied, "No one wants to be there tonight, Jack. People are dying. Now get some sleep." Percy then rolled to his other side.

Jack continued to stare at the flashes, pondering, until he drifted to sleep.

"Ahh! Why did you kick me!" Jack yelled as he jumped.

"Get up," Percy said while gathering his gear. "Sarge was through here five minutes ago, and I smell food. We need to get cleaned up and find that field kitchen."

Jack said nothing more as he stood groggily, grabbed his things, and followed Percy.

After breakfast, the Sergeant came back over to the troops. "All right, men. First group, clean your weapons now; second group, afterward. We do not want the Huns to catch us with all our weapons torn down. Also, confirm your ammunition amount, check your rations, fill your canteens, and inspect those gas masks for any cuts or cracks. And remember: if you are not cleanly shaven, your mask may not fit tightly."

These required tasks took time, but almost everyone was already prepared.

In late afternoon, the lieutenant came to the men and shouted, "Fall in!"

With haversacks and backpacks on, the troops shouldered their weapons and lined up in formation.

"Forward!" the lieutenant shouted, and the battalion began to move. They proudly paraded to the side of a dirt road as occasional groups of horsedrawn caissons, field guns, and trucks passed by. Soon, Jack noticed another group of soldiers coming the opposite way. They were headed to the rear on the other side of the road. As they passed, it was obvious they were the 'walking wounded.' Some were bandaged, others limped, some had cloth over their eyes and were being led by fellow soldiers, and many had a far-off stare in their eyes. None of them acknowledged the shiny new battalion headed to battle as they passed.

The sky began to cloud just before twilight when the battalion reached the outskirts of a deserted town. As they marched through the streets, it was obvious that the burned out and crushed buildings were validation that a great battle had taken place.

The troops marched on and were soon traveling a road that stretched through the fields east of town. It began to sprinkle just as the men reached the artillery line. The great guns sat silent under their canopies like sleeping beasts eerily waiting to be awakened so that they could fiercely attack.

Twilight had turned to darkness when the soldiers reached the beginning of a trench. The Sergeant sharply whispered to his group, "Keep your heads down in the shallow places or God may take you."

A soldier behind Jack mumbled, "If I get taken, God will have had nothing to do with it."

The troops traipsed through the mud of the zig-zagging trench until they were told to halt. A large group of soldiers were already there, huddling along the trench walls or in cubbyholes dug into its sides. Others just crouched down or stood. Jack and Percy found a place to lean just as it started to rain harder. Jack pulled his slicker out and put it on, hoping the raincoat's cotton twill would not soak through too quickly. Percy did the same before both men started their wait. The rain dripping from the rims of their helmets only added to Jack's anxiousness. He was again waiting for battle.

The rain quit at zero-two-hundred hours. Just afterward came the *puff, puff, puff,* of three flares launching. Like lanterns hung in the sky, the flares slowly floated down on tiny parachutes, illuminating the area around the trench and allowing the sentries to search for any enemy that may have crept in close. After the darkness returned, a five-man patrol slid over the top, on their bellies. Along with their rifles, each carried a large set of cutters to open access holes in the barbed wire. Just after they returned, an artillery barrage started, spooking everyone when the sudden loud blasts stole the quiet. Seemingly endless projectiles shrieked overhead before finding their mark with tremendous far-off explosions. It was chilling, yet comforting, to think that perhaps the enemy would be weakened by such power. Everyone, including the Germans, now knew a charge would come.

At zero-five-hundred hours the lieutenant came down the trench, shouting, "Stand to! Stand to!" The directive had everyone rushing onto the fire-step with guns pointed up the parapet wall. If an attack was going to come, it was usually just before dawn. The risk was greater yet if the enemy knew that there were inexperienced troops present.

A little over half an hour later, the lieutenant came back through, "Stand down, Stand down." He gathered his troops. "All right men: the Colonel says the bombardment will end at zero-six-hundred hours. That is when we go over the top."

Some men glanced at their wristwatches. It was twelve minutes away. The Lieutenant continued, "We are the first wave. Leave your backpacks here. You can take personal items and rations in your haversacks, but only the minimums. Check your belt, take the maximum amount of ammunition, have your first aid kit, and make sure your canteen is full. Once we are out of the trench and past the barbed wire, spread out, do not bunch up, stay crouched and alert, and keep moving forward. Machine rifle crews, I want you up front with the infantry to supply suppression fire. The heavy machine guns will stay back and give us cover fire. They will move ahead as our regiment advances. There will be battalions to our left and right flanks. Make sure your weapons are ready!" The lieutenant then walked away.

With so little time left, many soldiers rushed to fulfill the instructions. Others lit up cigarettes, some muttered prayers or nervously shook and even vomited from fright, while others just stood.

A chaplain came down the trench, stopping to pray with any man that requested him to. He reached the trembling soldier alongside Jack and began repeating the twenty-seventh Psalm. "The Lord is my light and my salvation; whom shall I fear? The Lord is the strength of my life; of whom shall I be afraid?" The chaplain then added, "God will be with you, son."

Jack overheard the words while pulling off his backpack and slicker. He rolled the items he was leaving behind in the raincoat and stuffed them inside the pack before finding a place to park it. Percy did the same while remarking, "Well, Jack, you got what you wanted."

"You too," Jack responded as he strapped the haversack to his chest.

"Not me," Percy responded. "I was conscripted."

Jack ignored Percy's remark as he double-checked his Chauchat machine rifle. He then asked, "Did you only load 16 rounds in each magazine and align them perfectly?"

"Yeah."

"Good. Maybe that will keep this thing from jamming."

Percy glanced at his watch. Three minutes. He shouldered his ammunition box and felt for the pistol in his holster. Jack grabbed the Chauchat in his right hand just as the command came. "Line up!" Then, the next command: "Fix bayonets!" The metallic sound of long knives being attached to gun barrels filled the air as the sergeant stepped a few rungs up on the trench ladder. He glanced at the troops before looking down the line at the lieutenant, who was standing on another ladder twenty yards away. The lieutenant was staring at his watch with his whistle in his mouth.

The barrage then ended with the last projectiles screaming overhead towards the enemy. The ensuing explosions echoed away until there was silence. Suddenly, the piercing shrill of the whistle shrieked. The exodus from the trench started.

With the sergeant leading, the soldiers filed up the ladders and out into the gray of the morning mist. Across 'No Man's Land', like ants, the large group maneuvered through the openings in the barbed wire and past the quagmire of mud and shell holes. Soon they were walking through an open field of high grass.

Where are the Germans? Jack wondered.

Many of the young soldiers had already forgotten their training. They began to bunch and walk, standing straight. Jack crouched, holding his gun with both hands while intensely searching. Percy followed alongside; his handgun drawn. The sergeant looked back to see some of the troops lackadaisically wandering. He fervently flung his arms around, trying to signal them to split up. Just then, a multitude of zipping sounds whizzed by. Soldiers fell as Jack and Percy dropped flat into the high grass. Jack flipped out the gun bipod and frantically looked. "There!" he shouted, spying helmets bobbing up from what must be a trench. He opened fire. *Boom! Boom! Boom! Boom!* The 30.06 caliber gun recoiled hard with every shot. *Boom! Boom! Boom! Boom!* He fired in bursts of four until all sixteen shells were expended. "Reload!" he yelled.

Percy yanked the empty magazine out and shoved another in. Jack instantly resumed firing as bullets continued to whiz through the grass. Two tanks came up behind the troops. Once in range, they opened fire. Their shells ravaged the German stronghold. Suddenly, enemy field artillery began a bombardment. Large explosions threw dirt into the air, dotting the field as deadly shrapnel cut its way in every direction. One tank exploded from a direct hit. The lieutenant knew the cannon fire would soon zero in on his troops. He spied shell holes ahead, left by the earlier American shelling of the enemy. He screamed, "Charge!" and ran forward.

A frenzied roar came from the soldiers as they followed. Men fell as rifles, machine guns, and mortars cut them down while artillery explosions tore apart anyone nearby. Jack jumped up and fired his gun from the waist while dashing ahead. Percy shot his handgun alongside him. All the firing weaponry of both armies created a deafening, constant thunder as the acrid smell and smoke of gunpowder owned the air.

Jack and Percy jumped into a shell hole alongside some other soldiers. Jack yelled again, "Reload!" Percy yanked out the empty magazine and slammed in a new one and Jack immediately fired.

The two armies were now so close that they could see each other clearly. Jack took aim at an enemy machine gunner and fired. The German's helmet flew off as he fell back out of sight. The guns kept firing as the sergeant stood up again and flung his arm forward. Troops crawled from the shell holes and advanced through the enemy's barbed wire, which had been torn to bits by the earlier shelling. Hand grenades flew in both directions before American soldiers jumped into the trench. Hand-to-hand combat started.

Jack and Percy ran through the wire barrier and up onto the trench wall. Jack looked right to see Germans coming down the trench. "Look out!" he yelled to Percy as he swung around and opened fire. *Boom! Boom! Click.* "Jam!" Jack screamed as he tried to rack the gun. Percy kept shooting his handgun. "Out!" Percy shouted, before wildly grabbing in his pocket for more bullets. Just then, other soldiers on top of the trench fired down on the Germans.

After a final rage the battle slowed, except for the sporadic sound of rounds being fired at fleeing Germans. Others raised their hands and fearfully shouted, "Kamerad!" (comrade), the word the Germans used for surrender.

Jack fell to his knees behind some timbers and continued to work on his jammed gun. Percy knelt alongside him and wiped the sweat from his brow as Jack shouted, "Keep an eye out!" Percy scanned the area before looking down into the trench—it was filled with broken bodies. He then glanced behind to the field. It was blanketed in the dead and dying. He could hear the anguished moans of the wounded. He heard voices crying for their mothers. He lowered his head, realizing the barbarity of what had taken place. Traumatized, he surmised, *We fight between the grace of God, and Satan's vengeance.* With a quiver in his voice, he then asked, "Jack, did you ever imagine this?"

"All I know is that we are still alive," Jack replied as he finally unjammed his gun. Instantly, he resumed watching for a counterattack.

"But . . ."

"But what, Percy?" Jack replied sharply, fearing Percy might say something that could conjure up thoughts of the slaughter he did not want to acknowledge. Jack finally calmed and said, "You had to realize that all those months of training was saying one thing: kill without remorse, or be killed . . . come on . . . I see our platoon regrouping over there."

Jack rose and started walking, Percy followed. Jack then saw a large shell crater to his left. He stopped and stared into the star-shaped hole. It held pieces of human flesh and blood. He instantly remembered the words old Mr. Regent, the one-legged veteran, had said years before about the crater at the nitroglycerin magazine disaster. It *did* look like war.

CHAPTER 19
Debut, the Student Army Training Corps, With a Ring

Mid-July 1918

Lucile and Earl's romance fully blossomed. Both families knew, but neither confronted the couple. Perhaps no one was willing to think of what tomorrow might bring.

Earl went about working the leases, continued practicing with the Odd Fellows Orchestra, and played his trombone with the Pleasantville Band. He spent every minute of his free time with Lucile. He received a letter from Arthur, addressed to everyone in the family. Arthur announced that he was taking basic training at Fort Slocum on Long Island Sound, New York.

Albert received another letter from Jack. Jack's regiment had been moved to the rear for some rest, which gave him time to write. What the censors did not scribble out were details about the battle he had been in.

Ella received a letter from her brother Romey, who was now in France. Romey was assigned duty as a saddler, responsible for repairing and maintaining saddlery and tack. The saddlers worked closely with the drivers of the battalion, artillery, and caisson wagons and also the cavalry. In his letter, Romey responded to Ella about Arthur. "I am so concerned about Artie," he wrote. "They always put the new cavalrymen at the front of a charge." His words struck Ella's soul. She cried for days.

Almon was still working the oil lease in Ohio, only able to come home every second weekend.

Albert continued to work for Universal Drilling.

The night of Earl's debut finally came. The IOOF lodge was packed with those who wanted to see the orchestra. Even Lucile's parents were there.

Every musician was ready, waiting for the conductor to raise his baton. With one flowing motion of his hands, the orchestra began to play. The acoustics of the hall and the sound of a full orchestra was astounding. Earl made an extraordinary effort, hoping that somehow it would culminate in approval from Lucile's parents.

The orchestra continued until there was only one composition left, 'Clair de Lune' by Claude Debussy. Earl put complete emotion into every note he played on the grand piano.

At the end, applause filled the building and standing ovations were taken by every member of the orchestra. Afterward, Earl rushed down the backstage steps and pushed through the crowd until he spied Lucile. He approached her from behind and lightly touched her shoulder. She turned, and her eyes lit up. "You were wonderful!" she said as she enthusiastically hugged him.

"Excellent!" Lucile's father said as he smiled and shook Earl's hand.

Earl then looked at Lucile's mother Elenore, who still wore a vague look on her face. She seemed to force herself to cordially say, "You did well." She then shook her head and said, "With your background, I find it remarkable that you can play so elegantly."

"Thank you," Earl said, alluding to the remark as a compliment.

Lucile instantly said, "Come home with us. I am sure you are famished, and . . ."

"I am certain that Earl must be getting home," Elenore interjected.

"Yes," Earl felt compelled to say.

"What time will you pick me up tomorrow?" Lucile asked as she concealed a wink from her parents.

"Oh yes," Earl remarked as he caught on. "I will be at your door at six."

"We are going to the movies, Mother."

The maneuver left Elenore no time to come up with an excuse for her daughter to stay home.

Earl finished work early that Saturday and, as promised, he knocked on Lucile's door at 6 o'clock.

"Hello," she said after opening the door.

"Hello," Earl replied.

Earl waited momentarily as Lucile stared at him. He finally said, "Shall we go? We can still catch the 6:20 trolley."

"No."

"No?"

"I am driving you in Daddy's automobile."

Earl was somewhat bedazzled by the thought of traveling in such a flashy car, but also felt a little uneasy, remembering how Lucile had driven when she came to see him in the field. But, soon, the couple was speeding down the dirt road that led from Pleasantville to Titusville. Upon entering town, the streets turned to brick, which made the auto ride even smoother. Lucile drove through the bustling traffic before finding a place to park. Then, hand in hand, they walked the crowded sidewalks to the Orpheum Theater. Earl stepped up to the ticket booth and asked, "What show is playing?"

"M' Liss', starring Mary Pickford," the clerk said.

Earl looked at Lucile, who shrugged. He noticed the line of patrons building behind them.

"All right," he said as he pulled the money from his pocket and paid her.

An usher escorted the couple inside and down the aisle, seating them a few rows back from the screen.

A few coughs came from the audience as everyone waited. Then the lights dimmed, and a news reel began flickering moving pictures of the war. A narrator, standing behind a curtain, started reading aloud from a prepared script.

"From Seicheprey, to Cantigny, to Belleau Wood, to Chateau Theirry, our troops are gallantly fighting for us all! The Huns know the Yanks are here with every bomb blast, every shot fired, and every charge! Our soldiers continue to push Kaiser's minions back to where they came from! But … we all need to help by buying Thrift Stamps, War Savings Stamps, and Liberty Bonds! Keep the caissons rolling!"

The patriotic fervor continued as images of soldiers, artillery, tanks, and horses all racing to battle crossed the screen. The bursting cannon fire poured onto the enemy as the gallant doughboys charged. The images ravaged Earl's mind. In his ecstasy, conscription had slipped from his thoughts. He could be taken at any time.

The silent film then started as someone began playing piano. The music added depth to the film and helped hide the clicking sound of the projector. The words of the actors flashed on the screen as Earl sat by Lucile in the dark, his mind continuing to ramble. *How will I tell her when it happens? Surely, she knows this.*

Lucile glanced his way, smiled, and said, "You are not watching."

Earl smiled back, sat up, and pushed his worries aside.

The next day found Earl working, as always, his mind wondering. Suddenly he remembered something he had read. *That is the answer,* he surmised.

Earl caught up on his work and, by Thursday forenoon, was on a train bound for Warren.

He disembarked at the station and briskly walked to the draft board building, reported in, then waited until a recruiter called his name.

"Have a seat, Mr. Ames," the man said. "My name is Lieutenant Elm Drougo. What can I do for you today?"

"I want to enlist."

"All right, let me pull your paperwork." Elm left and soon returned, holding a file. He sat down and began rummaging through the papers until he found the questionnaire. "What branch do you wish to enlist in?"

"I read in the newspaper that mechanics and engineers are desperately needed to work on all the new mechanized equipment. I want to enlist into the Student's Army Training Corps."

"You do know that there are qualifications?"

"Yes."

The recruiter read more of Earl's paperwork before remarking, "Huh. Your draft notice is slated to go out next week."

Earl said nothing.

Elm finally spoke up. "The army is lacking in educated personnel. That is why the Student's Army Training Corps was created. Men such as you are permitted to enroll in a university specifically for the purpose of joining the SATC. But you must meet the regular academic requirements of the university and the physical requirements of the army. Looking at you and your paperwork, I feel you are a prime candidate."

"Thank you, sir. When can I do this?"

"I can start the process right now," Elm replied. "Fort Pitt at Pittsburgh University is where you will be going—that is, if you pass everything. If you fail, you will immediately be put in the regular army. Also, if the army finds itself in desperate need of men, you will be called to fight."

"I understand."

The moment Earl finished, he dashed to the depot and boarded the first train bound for Titusville. Upon arriving, he went to Gardner Jewelers on Diamond Street. Afterward, he went home, grabbed all his old school tablets, climbed up into the barn loft, and began to study.

Sunday came. After church, Earl and Lucile made a picnic lunch and boarded the trolley to Titusville. Once there, they climbed on another trolley bound for Mystic Park. The summer sun flickered through the open windows as a warm breeze from the moving trolley gently caressed Lucile's flaxen hair. Her sunhat and parasol lay in her lap as they visited.

Upon arriving at the park, the two found it filled with people enjoying the beautiful day. The couple chose a private spot along Oil Creek and Earl spread a blanket over the sand. They sat down, Lucile opened the picnic basket, and they ate while nonstop conversation took over. Afterward, Earl rented a rowboat. They slipped off their shoes and soon were lazily floating down the creek. Earl, with his boater hat on, occasionally put an oar in the water to direct the vessel. Lucile, with her sunhat and parasol shading her, gazed at the slowly passing scenery. Earl finally flung the oars up into their holders and broke the silence. "These are not the words I want to say . . . but, I must tell you."

Lucile looked straight at Earl, waiting for what great secret he had to reveal.

"I . . . I joined the army."

Confused, Lucile's eyes began to mist as she sat up and asked, "Why would you do this?"

"Please, hear me out," Earl quickly replied. "I just knew that I was about to be drafted. That fear was confirmed when I went to the draft board on Thursday, so I joined the Student's Army Training Corps, the SATC. I will be stationed at Fort Pitt at Pittsburgh University. . . do you see? By train, I will only be five hours away, and after I complete basic training, I should be able to get leave to come home from time to time." He then added, "The army is going to pay for my education, and the war cannot last forever."

Lucile glanced away, trying to digest what she had just been told.

Earl sensed her uncertainty and immediately climbed over and embraced her. He gently kissed her, and she finally smiled.

This is the moment. He knelt on one knee, pulled a ring from his pocket, and said, "Marry me. . . whoa! Whoa!" *Splash!* He had lost his balance and fallen overboard. Lucile laughed hysterically as she looked on. All she could see was Earl's hat, floating wobbly on the water.

Another sudden splash, and Earl reappeared. He pushed his dripping hair back and grabbed the side of the boat with one hand. He opened his other hand—he still had the ring. "Marry me," he said again.

Lucile gazed at this drenched boy hanging on the side of a rowboat, asking her to spend the rest of her life with him. "Yes," she finally said as she leaned forward, and they passionately kissed.

Lucile held out her hand and Earl slipped the ring onto her finger. He immediately turned and began swimming away. Shocked, she called out, "Where are you going?"

Earl momentarily stopped and looked back. "To get my hat."

CHAPTER 20
The Meuse-Argonne Offensive

September 1918

J ack and Percy had first fought at Chateau Thierry and then through the battle for Saint Mihiel. Now they, along with what was left of their regiment, had loaded onto trucks and were enroute deep into Eastern France, to a place referred to as the Meuse-Argonne.

As they rode along, neither talked. Their crisp new uniforms were now dirty and frayed, their helmets scratched and dull. Jack looked at Percy and noticed the far-off stare in Percy's eyes—the look of tense and sustained combat. It was the same stare many of the wounded soldiers had displayed that day on the road.

As the convoy rolled on, the constant rumble of the motors seemed, in some peculiar way, to emit a sense of security. That false feeling was broken when the trucks veered around a host of shell craters, and a destroyed caisson wagon and two dead, bloated horses that lay along the road.

The trucks traveled on and soon were passing a continuous line of walking soldiers. Jack nudged Percy and said, "Look at those 'buck privates.' At least we get to ride."

Percy lifted his head to see all the soldiers and replied, "That only tells me that we will be in the first wave."

Jack did not know how to respond, so he pulled a hardtack from his pocket and forcefully broke it in two. "Here."

Percy glanced at the dry piece of biscuit in Jack's extended hand. He took it and remarked, "I now know why the army gave all of us a dental examination. You got to have good teeth to eat this crap without anything to soak it in."

Jack giggled, not because of Percy's remark, but maybe it was a sign that Percy was emerging from his despondency.

"Have you written home lately?" Jack asked, trying to extend the conversation.

"Yeah, I have a letter right here in my pocket. What about you?"

"I wrote my brothers yesterday."

"Brothers? I thought you said that you only had one brother."

"I do, but I also grew up with three others. I mean, they are friends, but I call them my brothers because we are that close."

Not much else was said as the trucks traveled on. After sixty miles the journey ended at a staging area behind an artillery line. After unloading and setting up camp, there was time to rest. Soldiers lounged, wrote letters, played cards, and washed their clothes and bodies. Some men stood around, joking and smoking; others slept. The field kitchens were in full operation. There was also something disturbing: more and more soldiers were taking sick and going to the triage.

Jack had noticed a few barrage balloons in the sky earlier. Curiosity prompted him to take a better look. After walking a distance, he put his hand to his forehead as a visor to block the sun's glare from his eyes. Squinting, he noticed a platform attached to one of the balloons. A soldier was in that platform. The man had his binoculars trained on something. Jack peered forward, glimpsing the silhouettes of swooping airplanes. He then noticed the far-off whining sound of their motors and the faint rattle of their guns firing. Too far away to tell which was the enemy, Jack marveled at the ballet of machines in the sky. As the dogfight continued, one plane started to go down, streaking the sky in ribbons of smoke until it crashed to the ground.

Suddenly, he jumped as the artillery line erupted with deafening blasts. The long row of howitzers fired in an orchestrated salvo; one gun's discharge immediately followed the next. Jack watched as a gunner hurriedly yanked open the gun breach, sending the empty casing flying out. The range-finder set the distance as the loaders rallied the next round into the cannon. The gunner slammed the breach closed and pulled the lanyard cord. The howitzer fired again in sequence. The crew already had the next shell prepared to repeat the process.

That was Jack's cue. He made his way back to the encampment, only to find more men and supplies arriving. That was when he noticed a group of large tents off by themselves. As he walked near, a fellow soldier stopped him and said, "You do not want to go any closer to those tents, friend."

"What are they for?"

"All our fellow soldiers who have the grippe."

"The grippe?" Jack questioned.

"The influenza…the Spanish Flu," the man replied. "Rumor has it that many of our boys are now coming off those crowded troop ships already sick. Some are dead." The man then pointed to a couple of stretcher bearers carrying a soldier. "That poor soul probably got sick on his way to this location, or after he got here. It seems as though the grippe is taking more of us than the Huns are."

Jack did not like the morbid statement. But it caused him to think back to the last battle Percy and he had been in. It seemed that more than the usual number of soldiers left the front line, sick. This was a threat that he had overlooked.

"Take care, my friend," the man said before he walked away.

"You too." Jack replied before he made his way back to Percy. He found him sleeping on a blanket alongside a tent. Jack sat down and spouted, "Hey, are you sick?"

Percy opened one eye and looked at Jack before saying, "No, but if you wake me again, I am going to puke all over you." Percy then rolled onto his other side and went back to sleep.

At zero-four-hundred hours, the troops were summoned to break camp and line up. The march started forward, past the artillery line and into the early darkness. The battalion halted after reaching a dugout area behind a long group of hills. The predawn light now allowed Jack to glance around at the many new faces. Just then, the sergeant came down the line. He approached his troops and began to issue his now-familiar instructions. This time, though, he had something more to say.

"Men, the lieutenant says that a major bombardment will start in…" he looked at his watch, "…fifteen minutes. It will last an hour. Then we will participate in a creeping barrage that will begin just on the other side of this hill. We will follow that barrage. It will advance by a hundred yards every three minutes. All troops that are up front, which includes us, need to stay back at least fifty yards from the shelling, in case any ordinance falls short.

"Now, listen closely. Do not get more than a hundred yards back, or those Huns that survive will have enough time to crawl out of holes and train their guns on you. The shelling will become a standing barrage at three hundred yards. That will guard against counterattacks while you and the rest of the infantry regroups and takes cover. The barrage may end there if the artillery is ordered to turn onto other targets." The sarge then made another comment. "We do not have a chaplain for this section, so we are left alone to our own thoughts and prayers."

"What happened to him?" a new recruit ignorantly asked.

The sergeant stared at the replacement before answering, "He was killed by a sniper last night."

The salvo started on time, just as the sarge had said. The far-off explosions ended an hour later. The sentries then came down the ladders just as Percy turned to Jack. "Here, take this." He stuffed his letter into Jack's shirt pocket.

"What?" Jack gasped as he reached for the letter.

"NO!" Percy shouted as he yanked Jack's hand back. "Listen! I will get it back from you later."

Jack was about to protest again just as artillery shells howled overhead and exploded just on the other side of the hill. The sound was horrendous – the ground quaked from the on-slot of continual exploding ordinance. The creeping barrage had begun. Clumps of dirt and pulverized rock flew back, raining down on the troops behind the hill. The commands of, "Line up!" and "fix bayonets!"

could barely be heard over the horrifying roar. The lieutenant climbed a few rungs up the ladder. He gripped his whistle tightly in his teeth as he hugged the hillside. He then lifted his arm to see his watch, while squinting his eyes as dirt and gravel bounced off his helmet. The sergeant climbed another ladder. He hunched his shoulders, trying to fit his whole body beneath the rim of his helmet, trying to shield himself from the rain of dirt. The earth downpour eased as the barrage started to advance. The sergeant kept glancing at the lieutenant, knowing the whistle would be almost impossible to hear.

Suddenly, the muffled shrill sounded as the lieutenant also hand-signaled to go over the top. The men began climbing the ladders, wondering if they were being led to certain death.

Once up top, the vast devastation was revealed to everyone, along with the ghastly sight of a continuous wall of exploding shells just ahead. Being only fifty yards back, everyone felt the concussion of the blasts. The landscape was being shredded. Shell craters were everywhere, the ground vegetation was pulverized and heaved into piles. Only the largest trees still stood, but they were now debarked trunks, with a few stubs where the largest branches had been.

In the smoldering smoke, the sergeant waved his arm and shouted as loud as he could, "Advance!" A few of his men that were close by, could hear and see the command, others noticed their fellow soldiers moving forward and began following the exploding wall of destruction. Jack and Percy maneuvered their way through the up-heaved terrain. *How could anything live through this?* Jack wondered as they continued for a few hundred yards. Suddenly, the rattle of machine gun fire came from nowhere. Through the sheets of smoke, chaos broke out as soldiers darted in all directions. Gunfire was everywhere. The carefully orchestrated attack had come undone.

"They are shooting at anything!" Percy screamed. In his confused state, he rushed forward, straight toward the barrage. *He will get too close!* Jack lunged, chasing Persey. The foot race ended when Jack caught Persey and pulled him down into a shell hole. Both men lay on their bellies with their heads down as dirt splattered over them. The earth shook as the barrage stopped moving. It was now a wall of unceasing explosions, the sound of which had culminated into one continual, deafening, thunder. *A semblance of hell* was the only description for such a horrific tactic.

Suddenly, it ended. The incessant sound echoed down a nearby valley until it was gone. Smoke, and the metallic smell and taste of gunpowder was all that lingered.

After a time, Jack lifted his head. The dirt fell from his helmet as he peeked over the top of the hole. Everything seemed eerily calm. Ahead, he noticed the lush green forest that had been left untouched where the barrage had stopped. He looked behind. There was nothing left. Everything had been destroyed. He then saw the helmets of his fellow soldiers popping up from behind what cover they had taken. He rolled back to Percy. "You all right?"

"Yeah," Percy replied.

The intensity of what they had just witnessed seemed beyond comprehension. Jack wiped his face with his sleeve before pulling out his canteen. He took a drink and then handed it to Percy, while muttering, "We need to hold here for a bit."

"Yes," Percy agreed as he took a drink. His hands were notably shaking as he handed back the canteen. "Jack . . . Sorry I lost control."

Just then came *thud, thud, thud,* and then a hissing noise. "What was that?" Percy anxiously asked. Jack glimpsed over the top of the hole to see a greenish-yellow cloud, "Gas!" he screamed. The two grappled for their gas masks and hurriedly pulled them on. Percy shouldered the ammunition case as Jack grabbed his rifle. They climbed from the crater just as the greenish-yellow death began creeping into it.

The sound of machine gun fire erupted, mortars exploded, as doughboys ran in all directions to escape the gas, and the bullets. Jack pointed ahead to a couple of tree trunks that were uphill, behind the death cloud. "There!" he screamed.

Both men ran as bullets hit the ground around them. They jumped behind the trunks as machine gun fire sprayed past their position. Jack flipped out the bipod of his rifle and began firing, but his field of vision was hampered by the mask. Percy blindly emptied his handgun just before a wave of doughboys ran past, attacking the machine gun nests head-on. Jack continued to supply suppression fire just as enemy artillery rounds started coming in. The explosions ripped the area apart. Jack and Percy covered their heads and hugged the dirt.

KABOOM! Jack sensed his body flying before he was slammed to the ground. Dazed, he lay there, gasping. The sounds of the battle were muffled by a high pitch ringing that screamed in his ears. He felt pain everywhere: his left arm throbbed and his eyes stung. He blinked, trying to clear his vision only to realize the Triplex glass eyepieces of his gas mask were fogged by his labored breathing, and speckled in red—one lens was cracked. He tried to get up, but instantly fell back as excessive pain streaked through his flesh. He turned his head. All he saw were the boots of fellow soldiers stepping over him, and running past. *They cannot stop; they have to fight.* He then focused on Percy, who lay with his back toward Jack. Percy's tattered shirt was soaked in blood.

Unable to call out, Jack could only faintly say, "Percy . . . Percy." But there was no answer; no movement. No one could hear him amidst the raging battle. *Stretcher bearer,* he cried out in his mind.

The *pain* was paramount. He raised his arm to glimpse through the battered lenses. A piece of shrapnel protruded through both sides of his forearm. Blood poured down his soaked sleeve. His breathing went shallow as his site faded—his arm dropped—his eyes closed.

CHAPTER 21
Letters from Camp Pitt

September 1918

Earl had passed all the requirements for the SATC and now stood at the Titusville train station, saying goodbye to Lucile, as well as the family members who could be there. Elenore was also present, her demeanor towards Earl softened by his upcoming studies at Pittsburgh University through the Student's Army Training Corps. Despite this, she had convinced Lucile to delay her marriage to Earl, citing the army's meager pay and Earl's financial needs. Beneath her reasoning, Elenore harbored a silent fear for her daughter—that, like the fate of others, the war could reach out and claim Earl.

After hugging his mother, Earl picked up Clara. The little girl proudly bragged, "Mama bought fabric! We are going to make a 'Sons in Service Flag.' It will have a red border, white background, and two blue stars in the middle—one for you and one for Artie."

"I am sure it will look very nice," Earl replied.

"Yes," Clara answered. "It is not as big as the one at church, but we will hang ours in the window for everyone to see."

"That is wonderful. Now give me a big, tight hug." Clara did so. Earl then sat her down and turned to Russell. Earl shook his hand as he said, "Be good, Russ. Keep Albo out of trouble and remember: I am depending on you to run the farm and the leases until I get back."

"I know. I will, Top," Russell replied.

The family stepped aside as Earl turned to Lucile. They

embraced for the longest time before she pulled back and said, "Hold out your hand."

Earl smiled curiously and did as Lucile asked. She pulled a wristwatch from her purse and clasped it to his wrist. She then looked into his eyes and said, "As you look at this watch, remember: it knows the time when you return to me." The two embraced again.

The train was about to leave. Earl passionately kissed Lucile, and then boarded. The whistle blew, the brakes released, and the chugging locomotive slowly began to move. Everyone waved as the train pulled from the station.

Earl stuck his head out an open window and waved until everyone disappeared. He then sat back in a seat and looked at the watch. Her words of longing and anticipation repeated in his mind. They were symbolic words he would never forget.

Hours later, the train stopped at Penn Station. Earl slung his bag over his shoulder and detrained. He stepped out from the station doors just in time to jump on a streetcar that was about to leave.

It was standing room only when Earl found a place to grab onto the overhead rail. That did allow him to easily peer out the windows at the smoky, bustling city. The Great War had made Pittsburgh a vital supplier of armor plate steel, cannons, and ammunition. This demand had swelled the city's population tremendously.

As the streetcar traveled, Earl noticed the menagerie of people on the sidewalks, both men and women. Some looked like immigrants, others like steel workers, and still others were businessmen. Some were richly dressed; others were clothed like paupers. A noticeable number of service men in uniform also dotted the crowd.

Where are they all going? he wondered. Earl also noticed the more-than-usual amount of random coughing coming from the streetcar crowd. He chalked it up to the soot of the city.

At the next stop he stepped off, lost and confused. He'd thought he knew where he was going, but obviously not. As he stood there, an army truck pulled up alongside him. The driver called out, "Hey, are you Earl Ames?"

"Yes. How did you know?"

"It was an easy guess. A young guy standing on the sidewalk, looking totally lost, with a bag of clothes thrown over his shoulder. You are the only one missing off my list. I did notice you at the station. I ran out to catch you, but you had already jumped a streetcar. Boarding this truck at the station was written in your paperwork."

Earl stood silent, not knowing what to say.

"Well, climb on, soldier."

Earl immediately stepped to the back of the truck's open bed full of recruits. One fellow reached out for Earl's bag as another helped him up.

Everyone was introducing themselves as the truck began to move. Soon they pulled onto a street that led between the stately buildings of the university. But these men were headed to the five hastily-built barracks that sat behind those buildings.

After a quick orientation speech by a major, everyone was sworn in and assigned a bunk. Inoculations and uniforms would come later. The cadets were then gathered for calisthenics. It was obvious there was urgency for this group to get fit and educated.

The rest of the week kept Earl busy. Basic training, drills, and his studies filled the hours. Over the rest of the week, he received a letter from Lucile almost every day. His parents and brothers also wrote—even little Clara.

On Monday, Earl noticed a posting on the bulletin board.

ATTENTION:

Tryouts for the army band

Assembly Hall

Friday September 13th

eighteen hundred hours.

Earl immediately wrote his mother and asked her to ship him his trombone. It arrived the day of the audition. Earl polished the instrument and blew it a little before heading to the hall. He won the position of first trombone. The same day, he received a letter from his mother.

Dear Son,

I hope you are fine. We are all fine here. After receiving your postcard, I sent your trombone out the next day. I hope you received it in time.

Here at home, we are working at the harvest. It is taking far longer and is excessively tiring because Albert, Russell, and I are the only ones left to do it, and Albert must work all day for Universal, beforehand. Little Clara does what she can. We dug the early potatoes yesterday. They are not very good, we only got fifteen bushels. The late ones are going to be much better. We got the oats all cut and stacked. The buckwheat is next. The corn stalks are over my head, but the cobs are still not ready. I hope the frost holds off until then.

Arthur has been writing frequently. I imagine he is writing you, also. The other day, I saw that recruiter who talked him into joining. He was standing on the sidewalk in Titusville. I wanted to go over and punch him in the nose, but your grandmother kept me from doing so.

We received a letter from Jackie Litzinger yesterday. He said he has been in two major battles and is enroute to another. He says he is all right, but I fear for him as much as I do my own sons.

I have been told that Clifford Schmidt was injured by gas. And now, on Thursday the twelfth, it was announced in the newspaper that every man eighteen to forty-five must sign up for the conscription. Albert will be eighteen soon, and says he is going to enlist right away. I beg of you, please write to him and tell him not to enlist. I have written Arthur with the same request. This family has already given so much to the cause with you, Arthur, your Uncle Romey, and Jackie, too.

I must get back to work now. Please write soon.

Love,
Mother

Inoculations came the next morning. Everyone stood in line as needles were pushed into arms. Afterward, many of the cadets became sick. Eight men from B Company passed out. A man named Jones, from Kittanning, collapsed and was taken to the hospital. He later died. Confused, Earl thought to himself, *"How can something that is supposed to protect you kill you?* A rumor spread that Jones was an alcoholic, and the vaccines are harder on them. Earl did not believe that because of what his grandmother had explained about his grandfather's alcoholism. Jones did not seem to have the identifying traits of an alcoholic.

The next day, Earl received a telegram from Arthur. It was a welcome distraction from what had taken place the day before.

Arthur wrote:

'HELLO TOP . . . I AM THROUGH BASICS . . . ASSIGNED TO 13TH CAVALRY . . . . TEXAS . . . WILL PASS THROUGH PENN STATION TOMORROW . . . EIGHT PM TRAIN . . . MEET ME . . . ARTIE.'

After reading the telegram, Earl said aloud, "I will be there, Artie."

Friday evening came. Earl was at band practice, and it was running overtime. He kept nervously checking his watch. He finally raised his hand and asked, "Sir, may I be excused? I must be somewhere soon."

The director looked at Earl and said, "Soldier, you are in the Army, now. You will be excused when we are finished. This band has many appearances coming up, and we will not blemish the Army's reputation!"

"Yes, sir," Earl replied. He then continued practicing.

Arthur's train pulled into Penn Station right on schedule. Dressed in his uniform, he scrambled off the car. His eyes flashed back and forth, searching for his brother. The large crowd of passengers began to diminish as he walked around the station. He stretched his neck and his eyes scanned everywhere. He finally returned to his car and waited. The minutes ticked away as a lump slowly formed in his throat. Top was not coming. He waited until the last minute, took one last look, and then climbed back on the train. It pulled from the station, and he was gone.

Finally, practice ended. Earl slammed his trombone into its case and rushed from the building. He glanced at his watch again as he ran. *Maybe the train was delayed.* That was something that happened from time to time. He then jumped a streetcar to the station. Upon arriving, he ran to where the trains were. He stopped in his tracks. The area was empty. It was between arrivals and departures. He ran to the ticket booth and asked, "Did the eight o'clock train from New York arrive?" The clerk looked at his paperwork before saying, "Right on time."

Earl's head dropped as he walked away. There would not even be an address to send an apology until Arthur reached his destination and contacted someone. Regret would haunt Earl until then. He traveled back to his barracks and finally drifted off to sleep.

The next morning was scheduled the same as most of the others. Calisthenics, drills, then studies, before the band headed to their first performance. He got back late, but still took the time to write.

Dear Lucile,

I have received all your letters. I am so sorry that I have been slow at answering them. It has been an extremely busy time, with basic training, my studies, and the Army band.

We played the evening of the twenty-sixth at Carnegie Music Hall before a crowd of three thousand. I have never heard such applause coming from that many people. It was deafening. Afterwards, a few people came up to me and said they had never heard a better brass band anywhere.

On Sunday we led the whole detachment (about eighteen hundred soldiers) down to Forbes Field for a Liberty Loan celebration. The American Federation of Musicians played. Their four-hundred-piece band created amazing music. There were some great speakers there, including a few wounded soldiers from France. I am certain Artie, Albo, and Jack would have loved to have been there.

Today, October first, we led a parade of the whole detachment, again, to the Allegheny Memorial Building. It was for a ceremony celebrating the turning over of the University of Pittsburgh to military training. We then marched ahead of the soldiers in review. I could never have imagined such pompous grandeur. Being a son of this time has allowed me to play a tiny part in this piece of history, but nothing compares to having your love.

We are supposed to play this Saturday at the Army verses Boston College football game at Forbes Field. That is, if it does not get canceled. Our band leader has warned us that it might because a flu has hit this area. We only had forty-two of fifty members able to play, today. Also today, the Pittsburgh Gazette-Times reported the city's first case of some influenza called 'The Spanish Flu.' They also reported that the area has been experiencing for weeks what they call an 'incipient grippe.' I feel fine though.

Well, I must close now, but I do look at my watch every day, waiting for the time when it tells me that I will see you again.

With love,
Earl

He wrote his address on the envelope.

Private, Earl L. Ames,
Headquarters Company,
Camp Pitt, Pittsburgh, Pennsylvania'

Afterward, he wrote letters to his family. A week later, Earl received a letter from Arthur.

Dear Top,

Hope everything is good with you. I finally arrived in Brownsville. Riding by train this far, I breathed in my share of coal smoke. All of us new guys are being held in quarantine for two weeks because of that influenza. Then we start training. I really missed seeing you at the station. I am certain it was something very important that kept you away.

I must tell you that since I left home, I have experienced many things. Fort Slocum is on an island. When I was there, I could look out and see mighty ships heading to sea. I swam in the Atlantic and saw seagulls and flying machines in the sky. I visited New York City and was amazed by its tall and numerous buildings. I saw some of the finest actors of our time on stage, and heard Arthur Guy Empey speak.

When I was ordered to Texas, they boarded us on a steamship to Jersey City. I saw bridges, ferryboats, and battleships. I then went by train across this nation. I passed through Pittsburgh, where you are, and then in Ohio I passed a few miles south of Bowerston, where Father is. I saw the Great Plains and the Mississippi River. I traveled two thousand miles to get here, but nothing equals seeing my family, and the farm on Goodwill Hill.

Duty calls. I must go now. Write me.

Artie

Arthur B. Ames

Recruit Detachment

13th Cavalry

Brownsville, Texas

Earl now had Arthur's address. He immediately sent a letter, explaining and apologizing.

CHAPTER 22
Tragedy of the Spanish Influenza

October 1918

The following week, Earl awoke with a terrible earache, but tried to ignore it and went about his day. That evening, a throbbing headache with an extreme burning fever began, drenching his body in sweat. His lungs felt heavy, making it hard to breathe. He reported on sick call to the infirmary. After a few days, he felt well enough to write.

Dear Mama, Father, and all,

I wanted to drop you a line to say that I am in the infirmary with a case of the Spanish Influenza. Now, do not worry, because I am getting along all right.

There is an epidemic of this disease, here. Camp Pitt has been quarantined. Also, the movie theaters and other public places have all been closed. I have been sick for three or four days now, and am quartered with seven or eight other fellows with the same disease. I do not know how long I will be here, but I suppose it will be until I get well.

We have a very good doctor, and are getting quality care. Another member of the band (his name is Harmon) is also here, so once I can get up and around, I will have company.

Do not worry, because I cannot complain, knowing what Jack and all the other fellows in France are going through I am better off here. Please tell Artie and the others. I will close now. Please write me at the following address.

> *Your loving son, Earl*
> *Private Earl Ames*
> *North Side Troop Infirmary*
> *Penn and Fifth Avenues*
> *Pittsburgh, Pennsylvania*

Earl then wrote to Lucile. Two days later, he wrote her again.

> *Dear Lucile,*
>
> *I am getting along, but have been moved to Magee Hospital now. It was recently commandeered by the military. I was moved here on the evening I last wrote you. So, if you immediately wrote back, I did not receive your letter. Write me now at the address at the end of this letter.*
>
> *I imagine I will be here until I get well. I had a terrible earache again this forenoon, but it has passed now and I am feeling somewhat better. This is a nice hospital and the nurses take good care of us, so do not worry. I look at my watch each day, and think of you.*
>
> > *With love,*
> > *Earl*
> > *Private Earl Ames*
> > *Magee Hospital*
> > *Forbes and Halket Streets*
> > *Pittsburgh, Pennsylvania*

Two days after receiving Earl's letter, Lucile heard a knock at her door. It was seven o'clock at night, so she looked out the side window first. The moment she saw who it was, she immediately opened the door. "Are you Miss Lucile Lake?" the man asked.

"Yes,"

"Telegram for you. Please sign here."

Lucile's shaking hand barely allowed her to sign her name. The man then handed her an envelope. She stared at it as the telegram messenger said, "Thank you." He then turned and walked away. A foreboding fear overtook Lucile as she opened the envelope and unfolded the message.

...FROM MAGEE HOSPITAL...PITTSBURGH...LUCILE...THIS IS MRS. CLARK ... EARL'S NURSE... HE HAS TAKEN A TURN FOR THE WORSE... YOU MUST COME NOW...

"Mother!" Lucile screamed.

Elenore came running into the parlor and saw the fear on her child's face. Tears were running down Lucile's cheeks as she handed the telegram to her mother while saying, "I must leave now. I must go to him."

Elenore glanced at the words of the telegram as she said, "But, child, you cannot. The last train has already left for tonight, and to go to him when he is sick with the influenza, would be a dangerous chance you take."

Lucile's voice crackled as she pleaded, "I have to, Mother . . . there must be a way."

Elenore could see and feel her daughter's anguish. She then thought of something, and stepped to the buffet. She pulled open the drawer, grabbed the train schedule, and quickly glanced at it. Elenore then flashed her eyes to the grandfather clock while saying, "If we leave in twenty minutes, we can still catch the night train to Pittsburgh at Oil City. Your father can drive us there in time—and I am going with you."

Lucile instantly turned and ran upstairs to grab some things as Elenore shouted for her husband.

Sometime later, Ella received the same knock at her door. As the telegram messenger walked away, he heard Ella scream, but the war, and now the influenza, had hardened his heart.

Clara, Russell, and Albert raced into the front room. Ella looked at them in silence as she faced the same dilemma. It was too late to catch the train. She regained her composure and said, "Children, Earl has gotten worse, and I must go to him. Russell, feed the animals early, then take Clara to Grandmother's house. You stay there with her."

Just then, Albert interrupted. "Mama, I am going with you." He then turned to Russell. "Russ, go to Universal tomorrow and tell my foreman, John Sparks, what has happened."

Russell shook his head yes just as Ella said, "Now, everyone get ready. We will leave before first light. That way, Albert and I can make the earliest train. And, children, pray for your brother." Ella then packed as her mind dwelled on Earl. All the recent news of the many people, including friends and even some relatives, who were sick or had already died from this dreaded disease, also raced through her thoughts. She had incessantly prayed for this plague to pass over her family, but it had not done so.

She went to the kitchen and pulled the cookie jar from the shelf, then poured what little money she had into her purse. Her mind raced. *Did Almon get the same telegram?* If so, he could get there earlier by train.

To save time at the telegraph office, she wrote down what she would send to Arthur. 'My son, Arthur—Earl has taken for the worse. I am enroute to him. Dear child, grid your soul, prepare for the worst and pray for the best.'

Elenore and Lucile made the night train. As the click-clack of steel wheels rolling on the rails echoed through the car, Elenore closed her eyes while Lucile stared out the window at the darkness. Her mind was consumed with thoughts of Earl as she pummeled herself. *Why did I take so long to accept his love? What was I so afraid of? He is the one. And now, I could lose him.*

The train arrived at Penn Station just before dawn. Elenore and Lucile detrained before boarding a jitney to Magee Hospital. Upon arriving, they quickly walked to the door, but a soldier was guarding the entrance. "Sorry, ladies. This is a quarantine building; you cannot enter," the man sternly said.

"But we must!" Lucile protested. "We were summoned by Nurse

Clark to come here to see Earl Ames."

The soldier blocked the way, holding his rifle across his chest while staring at Lucile.

Lucile broke into tears and pleaded, "Please, sir. He is my betrothed and there may only be a short time."

The soldier's heart went out to Lucile as he seen the tears in her eyes and felt the anguish in her words. "Wait here," he said as his conscience shouted, *today again, am I allowing more people to pass to their graves*? He went inside. Soon, he came back with two gauze masks and a pass that read,

> Subject: Earl Ames.
>
> Admit: Relatives.
>
> To: Ward 2C.

The small piece of paper was signed at the bottom, R.R. Hendershott, Captain, M.C.

"Take the first staircase to the left," the soldier stated as he pointed. "Ward 2C is then straight down the hall."

"Bless you," Elenore said to the guard before Lucile and she made their way to the second floor. As they walked the corridor, recruits on cots aligned the full length of the hall. Coughing and moaning were the only sounds other than the tapping of Elenore's cane on the tile floor, and the clicking of the two women's shoes as they walked. Nurses, dressed in white and wearing face masks were the only others they passed.

The women finally reached a double door that led into a wide, long ward. The filled beds were set on an angle. There was a triangular folded sheet hanging between each one. Lucile looked at the face of each man she passed until she spied Earl. She immediately slid in alongside Earl's bed and stared at him. His forehead was beaded with sweat, his hair was matted and tangled, his breathing was erratic, and his complexion had a bluish tinge. A nurse brought over a couple of chairs and then introduced herself. "Hello, I am Nurse Clark. You must be Lucile?"

Lucile could only nod as the nurse turned to Elenore. "And you must be Earl's mother?"

"No, I am Lucile's mother. But I feel certain Mrs. Ames will be here soon. Thank you for contacting us, and thank you for the chairs."

Earl, recognizing Elenore's voice, opened his eyes. Through his clouded vision, he noticed Lucile's silver-blue eyes above her mask. He tried to talk, but Lucile shushed him. "You need all your strength to get well. We will have plenty of time to talk later."

Nurse Clark then looked at Lucile and Elenore while saying, "I am sorry we have had to meet under these circumstances, but I am glad that you are here. Earl has been with us for six days now. He is extremely weak and has a terrible cough and widespread pain, especially in his left ear. Yesterday his temperature spiked so high that delirium set in. The only thing we could do was strip him down to his skivvies, put a damp sheet over him, and then roll him outside onto the veranda. We have done that with many patients. The cold did lower his temperature some. Hopefully he got a good dose of fresh air … well, in this city, smoky fresh air."

The nurse then looked directly at Lucile and with an expression of great concern on her face added, "Although he has not said much, when he does, it is always of you, his family, and some wonderous place called Goodwill Hill."

The nurse's words brought little comfort after such a dismal diagnosis.

"Thank you," Lucile replied, trying to control her emotions.

The nurse then nodded and left to attend other patients as the hospital was filled beyond capacity, and was understaffed.

The two women sat in the chairs, distressed and exhausted. Hours passed as Earl's breathing became more labored. From time to time he would cough, but the sound of his coughing became gravellier as the time passed. Nurse Clark then returned with a cold compress and gently wiped Earl's forehead. She noticed speckles of blood across the pillowcase, caused by Earl's coughing. There was blood running from his nose. She dabbed it away before getting a clean towel to lie over his pillow.

(At this time in history, antiviral drugs and antibiotics had not yet been developed. There were many unproven, sometimes bazaar, home remedies. But the hospitals had not much more than supportive care. At times, they tried quinine, blood transfusions, strychnine, and even creosote, along with aspirin, epinephrin, salicin, camphor, castor oil, and a few other compounds. There was nothing available to fight one of the deadliest viruses in modern history.)

Finally, Almon arrived. He nodded to Elenore and Lucile before touching Earl's leg while saying, "I am here, son." There was no recognition from Earl.

Another hour passed before Ella and Albert arrived. They acknowledged everyone before Ella leaned close to her son and softly said, "Earl, my child, Mama is here." She then took her hand and gently pushed back Earl's hair, like she had when he was small. She hoped that, in some way, her touch might comfort Earl, and perhaps he would miraculously get better.

"Top!" Albert spoke up. "It is Albo, Top. I am here." Again, no answer.

Earl lay motionless for an endless time as all his loved ones looked on. Finally, his eyes slowly opened. He looked directly at Lucile as she stared back. A glimmer of hope filled Lucile's heart as she stood from her chair. Though swollen and bloodshot, Earl's eyes still seemed to resonate the love he held for her. He then exhaled— his eyes closed forever.

"NO!" Lucile screamed as she flung herself onto Earl.

"Lucile!" Elenore cried out. "You cannot! You cannot!" She pulled Lucile back while bursting into tears. Her voice broke up as she struggled to say, "my child . . . my child." She held on tightly to her daughter as grief overwhelmed everyone.

Ella held Almon tightly as they wept in each other's arms. Albert put his hands over his face to hide his tears as he shook in grief. Unimaginable pain shot through their souls.

After a time, Almon lifted his head, looked at his son's lifeless body, and through his sorrow solemnly said, "He now belongs to God's will . . . and our memories."

There were tears in Nurse Clark's eyes as she checked Earl before doing what she had done many times before. She gathered the family and led them to a room while the grief continued.

After some time, an officer stepped into the room, pulled down his gauze mask and introduced himself. "Hello, my name is Captain Hendershott. I am commander of this facility. Please accept my condolences for your loss. Private Ames was a fine soldier who stood out among his peers." The captain paused before stating, "Nurse Clark told me she had summoned all of you here in hopes the visit might help Private Ames. She is one of our best nurses, but at times her heart throws caution to the wind." The Captain then paused before continuing, "I know there is never a right time to talk of this, but because of the current crisis I will have your son's body ready to travel by tomorrow."

"What are you going to put him in?" Ella quickly asked.

"The standard issue transport box."

"No!" Ella cried as her tears flowed again, "I will not have my son in a pine box! Where do I buy a casket?"

"There is nowhere. I am fortunate just to be able to supply a box."

"What do you mean?" Ella asked in surprise. "In a city this large, you are telling me there are no caskets to be had?"

"Yes, ma'am," the captain replied. "There is a good-sized population, here, but that is the problem. This city is in turmoil, the likes of which no one has ever seen before. Scores of people are dying each week now, and of the local companies that make caskets, many of their employees are either off sick, or have died." Hendershott paused, and then continued, "Pittsburgh did have two train carloads of caskets destined to arrive last week. They were coming from down south where this plague is not as prevalent. But some man named Louis Brownlow, the city commissioner of Washington D.C., hijacked those cars for his jurisdiction. He took them, and left Pittsburgh with none." (reference: 'How America Struggled to Bury the Dead During the 1918 Flu Pandemic' by Christopher Klein. www.History.com)

You could sense the discouragement in the captain's voice before he stated, "I am certain that he needed those coffins just as badly as we do." Hendershott then said, "The Red Cross, the Eagles, and the Lions Clubs are working to get more caskets, but it will take time. I do not think you would want your son's body setting in some temporary morgue until then."

Ella, lost for words, turned her head and wiped her eyes with the handkerchief she carried. Almon spoke up. "All right, then."

The following morning, four soldiers carried Earl's remains through the train station. They set the pine box down and stood by it while a few workers set up a ramp to an empty boxcar. Lucile walked over and the soldiers stepped back. She stared at Earl's name, company, section, and regiment, which were stenciled across the top of the box. Her eyes welled with tears as the realization that he was gone, set in deeper. She finally stepped aside. The soldiers picked up the box and loaded it into the car. All four soldiers then saluted Earl's body, but only three walked away. The fourth soldier had stayed inside. Almon and Ella walked to the box car's still-open door and looked in. The soldier was just standing there.

"What is your name, son?" Almon asked.

"Sergeant Harry Engel, sir.

"Well, Sergeant Engle, you can go. One of us will stay back here with Earl."

"No, sir. I have orders to escort a fallen brother-in-arms home. Besides, I volunteered for this. Your son was my friend."

The statement tugged further at Almon's heart. His voice crackled as he replied, "I understand."

The train ride home was somber. Albert sat by himself, watching the scenery pass as the sunlight flickered through his window. His mind recalled all the times, good and bad, that he had spent with Top. It seemed as if those moments had all happened just yesterday. Now, the memories he had gathered would be where he visited his brother forever.

Arriving at Titusville, he found that the news of Earl's death had already been published in the Titusville Herald Newspaper.

Members of the Queen City Guards were there to unload the body and transport it to the family home. At the house, Almon and Albert set up two sawhorses in the front room before Ella and Clara spread the best tablecloth they had over the top. Earl's box was then placed there.

Almon looked at Ella. "I have to leave."

"Where are you going?" Ella asked.

"I just have to leave."

"I will go with you," Albert said.

"No, son. I have to go alone."

Almon then went to the barn, hooked Prince to the wagon and rode away. Ella worried as she watched Almon disappear down the road.

It was dark when Almon returned. He pulled the wagon up close to the house and said, "Whoa, Prince." He then went inside to see Ella sitting in the old rocking chair, staring at Earl's box.

"Albert, Russell, come here," Almon called out.

The boys came down the steps from the bedrooms upstairs and looked at their father.

"Get your boots on. I need help."

All three went outside as Ella continued to stare at the box. Soon they came back in, carrying a shiny new casket and set it down on the floor. Ella's red eyes brightened some as she looked at Almon and said, "Get our son out of that box."

No one ever asked Almon where he had gotten the casket. It did not matter.

The funeral service was held at the house at two o'clock the following day. The small attendance was only because of the restrictions placed on gatherings. Reverend David Sleppy, of the M. E. Church, officiated. All of Earl's family was present, except for Arthur. Elenore and Lucile were also there. Flowers and cards came from everywhere. Even people unknown to the family sent condolences. The Queen City Guard of Titusville again supplied their services and moved the casket from the house to Cheney

Cemetery. As they lowered Earl down into the grave, the finality set in. The Reverend's words faded into a distant murmur as Lucile stood—tears brimming in her eyes. The others held back when she stepped to the edge of the grave—her sorrow so deep, she just stood there, motionless. The pleats of her black dress slightly flowed in an ever-so gentle breeze before she dropped the flowers she held. They fell across the casket. Ella then did the same before stepping over to Lucile. She opened her arms and embraced Lucile for the longest time. Not a word was spoken as the two women then walked together, away from the gravesite. The others followed. Almon carried Clara as she cried in his arms. Two men with shovels then began their task—no one looked back—the pain was too great.

Later that night, Ella wrote Arthur.

> *My dear son,*
>
> *I prayed I would never have to write you these words. Earl did not survive. I know this is tearing your heart apart right now as it has all of us. But, take comfort in the fact that he lived a good life—and if there is a reward in that, Earl has earned it.*
>
> *We laid him down in Cheney, just above your grandfather. It was a small ceremony only because of the restrictions. I will write you a longer letter soon.*
>
> *I know the influenza is everywhere now, but around here it seems as though everyone is either sick or dying. Son, if they give you furlough, I beg of you—Do Not Come Back Here. There will be a future time for us to grieve together.*
>
> *Your loving mother*

Her tears stained the envelope as she sealed it.

CHAPTER 23
The Aftermath

October 1918

A few days had passed since Earl's funeral. Life had to now go on without him. Albert struggled through his depression to find the energy to get dressed for work. He finally saddled Prince and made his way to Universal's office.

As he opened the office door, John Sparks jumped from his chair and yelled, "Stop! You cannot come in here, Albo!"

Astonished, Albert asked, "But why?"

John looked Albert straight in the eye and said, "Because of what your brother Russell and the newspaper told me. I read that you were down to Pittsburgh with your brother Earl when he passed. You have been exposed, and I cannot take the chance of you spreading that disease to the other men."

Astonishment still clung to Albert's face as he pleaded, "But, John."

John lashed back, "I am sorry, Albo, that is all I have to say. Now, you need to leave."

Albert stared at John before he shook his head slightly and closed the door. He walked back to Prince and untied the reins from the hitch rail. He slowly led the horse as the pain was too great to ride. Tears ran down his face not just because of a confrontation with someone he had looked upon as a friend, but because Earl's death was too fresh. Besides, all that John had displayed was uncontrolled fear.

Shep howled out his usual greeting just as Albert and the horse stepped off the road. Upon reaching the house porch, Albert tied Prince to the railing. Shep instantly sensed the sadness and timidly wagged his tail. Albert reached down and gave the dog a pat on the head just before he entered the house.

After telling his mother, Albert went back outside and led Prince to the barn. He unsaddled the horse and then went looking for Russell. There would be lots of things that Russell would need help with, and keeping busy was the best answer.

Every day, the paper brought more notices of sickness and death from the influenza. Also listed were those wounded and killed in the war. Public events and meeting places, including all churches, schools, and theaters, were closed. The rules were: no spitting, and use a handkerchief to cough or sneeze in. Many people wore masks, and for anyone who had to travel, the train and trolley car companies had been ordered to block all the car windows open. The newspaper advised to also keep house windows open. If anyone felt sick, they were to go to bed immediately.

Along with all the home remedies, the drugstores carried a multitude of products from camphor gum to mustard ointment to spices to make Poultices. Pneumonia salves, influenza tablets, salts of quinine, special laxatives, and a host of other merchandise were sold as remedies.

As these concoctions failed to make a difference, the influenza continued its deadly rein. (During the Spanish Flu Pandemic of 1918, Pennsylvania became one of the states with the highest mortality rate in the nation.)

One night, there was a knock at the door. Ella jumped from her bed, wondering *Who could that be at this hour?* She ran to the stove and lit a lantern. Albert joined her, and together they opened the door. There stood a young woman, sobbing. She immediately cried out, "Mrs. Ames, I hope you remember me. I am Ruth Dane's daughter, Anna. I live in Grand Valley now."

"Yes, I remember you. Your mother told me that you had married."

"Yes," Anna replied, "but I am in desperate need of help. My husband and three stepchildren are all terribly sick with the influenza. I contacted Doctor Proper, but he is overwhelmed. There are few other doctors available because so many left for the war. And those who are still here are also too busy to come. My mother is sick herself, and is still caring for my father since that bull attack. My other relatives and neighbors are either sick, caring for their own sick families, or are too afraid. I do not know what to do, or who else to turn to. Please, help me."

"Come inside, child," Ella said.

"No, I must get back," Anna quickly replied.

Ella, somewhat confused, then asked, "Why did you come to me?"

"My mother told me you are a good person and that you were with your son when he passed. You were exposed and have not gotten sick. That is why I am here."

The mention of Earl caught Ella off guard. She paused, then muttered, "I will get my things."

Just before Ella left, she turned to Albert and said, "Take care of Clara and keep track of Russell. Your father should be home tomorrow. Tell him where I am."

"I will, Mama."

Almon arrived the next day. Albert talked with his father for a bit, telling him the news. Afterward, Albert went to get the mail. As he opened the box, a few letters stood out from the other mail. He pulled out one. It was from Lucile, addressed to Ella. Albert snuck a look at it. Everyone in the family read each other's mail—besides, his father was home. Ella would suspect him first. He quickly scanned the pages as a few sentences stuck out. 'I came down with the influenza just after Earl's funeral. I paid for the terrible risk we all took by going to see him. Although I was deathly sick, if he was still here, I would gladly take that risk again. My mother came down with it, also, but not as badly. Thankfully, we are both beginning to feel better now.'

Then, another statement rose off the page. 'I know you did not think I was worthy of him. All I can say is that you are not the only one who loved him, and you are not the only one who has lost him forever.' The sadness was too great. Albert refolded the pages and slid them back into the envelope.

On the other envelope, he immediately spied the now familiar words 'soldier mail' written in the upper right corner and, on the lower left side, the blue, round ink stamp of the censor. He opened it and began reading.

Hello Albo,

I received your letter a while ago. I imagine you have been wondering why I had not written back. Well, I can tell you what happened, now, because the censors allow us to say more.

We were fighting in the Argonne forest when a large-caliber round exploded nearby. The next thing I know is that I woke up here, in this field hospital. I am told that it is in some French town named 'Tours.' I guess that I have been here for about two weeks or more.

The shrapnel busted me up pretty bad. My buddy Percy was closer to the blast. No one knows if he made it, but he is not here. I pray that he is not still lying out there. I have seen that. Another thing bothers me: he stuffed a letter in my pocket just before we went over the top. I do not know what it said. It was missing from my belongings when I came to.

Right now, my left arm is useless, but I feel it will heal up quickly so that I can get back to help my buddies. But this doctor tells me not to get my hopes up. He says the best I may get is to be listed B-2—not good enough for the front, but able to work at something in the rear.

Anyway, I had to laugh when you mentioned in your one letter about the time when we were kids and were sent to gather chestnuts. I will always remember when we started throwing them at each other. Boy, those spiny hulks hurt when they hit you.

I hope all of you are well back home. I imagine Top and Artie have come over by now. Please send me their addresses so that I can write them. My address is on this envelope.

Tell everyone you have heard from me, and that I am all right.

Jack

Jack does not know, Albert realized as he grabbed the rest of the mail and walked to the house. He immediately sat down and wrote back.

Jack,

I am so sorry to hear of you getting wounded. I am so glad that you survived. You are tough as an old goat, and I am certain that you will heal up just fine. I am also sorry to hear of your missing buddy.

That battle must have been a bad one. I imagine that you were right in the thick of it.

From what you replied to in your letter, it is obvious that you never received the other letter I sent.

I must tell you some things. First: Artie is stationed with the 13th Cavalry in Texas, along the Mexican border.

Top asked Lucile to marry him just before he was stationed with the SATC at Camp Pitt in Pittsburgh.

The Spanish Influenza is everywhere, now. There are sick and dying people all around us. Most everything is closed.

Anyway, I do not know how to tell you this, so I am just saying it outright. Top got that influenza and did not make it. His loss has left all of us heartbroken.

With Earl being my brother, I failed to realize just how accomplished he was, and how many people he had touched, until I seen all the condolences and read a special Pleasantville news article about him in the Titusville Herald. Among the many things written was the statement that Earl was 'one of the most estimable young men this community has ever known.' (Titusville Herald Newspaper, October 22,

176

1918, Page 3.)

I know that he thought of himself as just a country farmer who pumped oil leases and played trombone and piano. He loved Lucile and his farm on Goodwill Hill, but he was more than that.

I have included Artie's address. This is all I can write for now. Please write back soon and let me know how you are doing.

Albo

He then wrote to Arthur.

Dear Artie,

How are you doing old weasel hunter? I hope you are well. I know that Mama has already told you about Earl. He will live on in all our hearts until we are gone. The church changed his star to gold on the Sons in Service Flag. Mama cannot bring herself to do that yet on our family flag. All I can say is that you are the eldest now, so you are 'Top'.

Anyway, we have heard false rumors of the war ending, but every time that happens, it tortures the mothers and wives who are waiting for their soldier boys to come home.

I have heard the Spanish Flu is not as bad in the south and where you are. It is all around us here. The whole Billings family caught it and their daughter died. Jess Stevenson has it bad, and so does Leon Osborn. Joe Henderson, Nellie's brother, died of it last week. Frank Lindquist died yesterday. He was only sick for three days. Lucile is just starting to get over it. I guess her mother is getting better also.

My foreman John fired me because of my being down to see Earl when he passed. He said I was exposed, and he was too afraid I would pass the sickness to everyone. He is wrong. Neither Mama, Father, nor I are sick. But Mama is right: you are safer where you are.

Jack wrote me. He was wounded, but says he is healing. Enough of all this sadness now. I gathered a bunch of stones from the edges of the fields and dumped them in the corral. I am pounding them all in flat, to get rid of those muddy places. I put out the trapline and hope to catch a bunch of weasels, but the bounty price is still the same, and everything is so much more expensive now. There does not seem to be many rabbits this year, but a lot of squirrels. I wish you were here to hunt them with me.

So, tell me: now that you are in the cavalry, have they taught you what each end of the horse does?

Your brother,
Albo

Twelve days later, Albert received a letter from Jack.

Dear Albo,

I received some mail last evening and got your letter. I was shocked to learn about Top. There is nothing I can say that will lighten this. But, allow me to express my heartfelt sympathy.

Earl gave his life for his country. There is no difference whether he served back home or faced the guns here in France. We will remember him as a soldier and the gentleman that he was.

I thought of him as a brother. Your loss is also mine. Tell your mother and father that I am so sorry. How sorry, I cannot express in words.

Jack

CHAPTER 24
The End of the War

November 11, 1918

It was 3 AM. The ticking wall clock was the only sound in the office of the Petroleum Telephone Company. Miss Mina Chase, the night operator, barely held her eyes open. Suddenly she was startled by an incoming call. She pushed the cord into the board and said, "Operator."

Through the static-filled line a muffled voice relayed the message everyone had been waiting for. Excited, she shouted, "Yes! Yes! I will! I will!"

She hung up and instantly called the mayor, but there was no answer. She then called the school principal—no answer, again. She started calling every church in town. Finally, Reverend David Sleppy, in a groggy voice, answered. "Hello."

"Reverend Sleppy, this is Mina Chase, the night operator. Thank goodness you picked up! I must tell someone, and no one else answered their phone. The war is over!"

"What?" the reverend cried out, trying to make sure he had heard right.

"The war is over! The powers that be signed an armistice, and the fighting stops at 11 AM, Paris time! That is 5 AM here. How do we let everyone know? You are the only one who has answered their phone."

"I know exactly how," the reverend replied. He was so excited that he hung up the phone without saying goodbye. He threw on his clothes before waking his wife. "Dear, I must go to the church.

Answer the phone every time it rings and say, 'The war is over.'"

"It is the middle of the night," his wife protested. But the Reverend never heard her. He was already running down the stairs.

He reached the church, yanked open the door, and ran to the rope. He gave a great tug, and the bells began to ring. He rang and rang the bells.

The phone began ringing at the parsonage, Mrs. Sleppy did as her husband had asked. Each time it rang, she picked up the receiver and said, "The war is over."

Soon church bells were ringing all over Pleasantville. Someone was even ringing the school bell. The far-off sound of Titusville's church bells ringing could be heard in the distance.

By 5 AM, the entire village had been aroused and the American flag was hoisted in the public square. By 7 AM, a bevy of schoolchildren had gathered with horns, bells, drums, and even tin pans. A group of enthusiastic adults formed an impromptu parade and marched up Main, Merrick, Chestnut, and State streets.

Mayor Jack Dack issued a request for all businesses to put out their flags and close by noon. The Red Cross hastily met and planned a grand parade to start at 4 PM (the event was reported on by the Titusville Hearld Newspaper the next morning, November 12, 1918, Page 6.)

Albert was pulling a few hay bales down from the loft when he heard an automobile pull in. He stepped outside, straining to see until his eyes adjusted to the light. It was Lewis Watson, walking his way. When Lewis was within speaking distance, he called out, "Hello, Albo."

"Hello to you, Mr. Watson. What brings you out here today?"

Lewis took his last few steps to Albert and said, "Did you hear the bells?"

"Yes, but I do not know why they were ringing."

"Because the war is over."

Albert stood dazed. He then said, "I have to go tell Mama!"

"Wait," Lewis said. "Pleasantville is having a parade, starting at

4 o'clock today. I know this is short notice, but the band is going to lead this historic event and I need every member there. Our ranks are thin compared to what they once were."

"But, what about the influenza? And the mandates against congregating?" Albert questioned.

"Albo, this local area, and for that matter, the whole nation, has been praying for this day to come. The suffering has been tremendous for so many families. Today's celebration is not just about the war's end. It also marks the start of healing—something we all need. This is worth the risk."

"I will be there," Albert responded.

"We meet at town square," Lewis said. "Try to be a little early. Now, I must get going. I have other members to contact." Lewis then shook Albert's hand before he walked back to his auto and left.

Albert ran to the house to tell his mother and gather his uniform and trumpet.

He arrived just in time. The parade line was already forming. As he walked from the back of the parade forward, the last in line were the many Service flags from the churches, mixed in with numerous American flags. Next were the Red Cross workers, dressed in their uniforms of white caps and aprons. The school children were aligned in rows, each one holding a small American flag in one hand and a little horn to blow in the other. Albert counted twenty-eight automobiles loaded with parents who had sons in the service. Ahead of them was a single automobile carrying three civil war veterans, all dressed in their uniforms. That auto was flanked on both sides by the Boy Scouts.

He reached the band and took his place. As he stood there, he realized what Mr. Watson had said. The band was missing many of its members. He looked right, thinking, *Artie should be here, asking, 'Are you ready, Albo?'* He glanced to his left. *Jack should be there, standing straight as a toy soldier.* He then turned to look at the row behind him. *Top should be there, giving me a big smile while saying, 'Turn around, Albo.'*

Just then, Mr. Watson raised his hands and the band made ready their instruments. He dropped his arms and turned as every member marched in place and began to play. Lewis marched forward as the band followed in step. Albert played as loud as he possibly could, never missing a note. He was playing not just for himself, but for his brothers and Jack.

The crowds on the sidewalks cheered as the parade began to move, announcing a message of peace and of the great joy that one of the darkest times in American history was ending.

(Unfortunately, tens of thousands of sons, fathers, and husbands were not coming home. In the nineteen months that American soldiers fought in World War One, an estimated 116,500 died, including over 400 American women who died overseas in various supporting roles from nursing to telephone operators.

Many of the wounded, like Jack, spent more time overseas before they had healed enough to make the journey home.

As part of the terms of the Armistice, an occupation force which included 16,000 experienced American soldiers was immediately stationed in Germany. That force stayed there for almost four years.

The Spanish Influenza's reign would continue for over a year longer than the war, eventually taking an estimated 675,000 American lives.)

CHAPTER 25

U.S. 13th Cavalry as a Death Occurs

November 1918

The hot Texas sun beat down on Arthur as he, along with three hundred other men of the 13th Cavalry, saddled up and trained in the big field with the large circle marked out in the middle. That circle was called the 'bull pen.'

The training always included instruction on how to properly mount and dismount and how to sit in the saddle (called the 'military seat').

"Fours right about!" the trainer shouted, and the cavalrymen, aligned in fours, turned the trotting horses right until they were headed back from where they had come.

"Right front into line!" The riders to the right moved forward and inwards to form a single line.

The next mounted drills were tougher, and although the whole cavalry performed these, there was a specialized group that received further training in equitation, which included other drills. They were called 'Skirmishers,' and Arthur was one of them.

The Skirmishers were a select group of light cavalry that was embedded within the full cavalry unit. This group could be deployed separately. They were trained to operate in more random, spread-out formations. The Skirmishers were used for special operations such as rear guard, flank guard, and vanguard positions. They were also used for strike and flight actions to harass and delay the enemy and to lead shock charges. The Skirmishers were used for any action that a heavy cavalry unit might not be suited for.

The next mounted drill of the day was: at trot, take your feet out of the stirrups, raise your knees above the pommel, and touch them together.

Second drill: at walk, swing your arms above your head while twirling as far left and right as you can.

Then came the command "Scatter!" Everyone yanked their reins and galloped their horses in different directions.

Finally came "Halt down!" Every man instantly stopped his horse and grabbed his rifle from its sheath, while dropping from the saddle. Landing belly-first onto the ground, the soldier had his gun cocked, aimed, and ready to fire.

All the horses were taught not to spook or flinch when gunfire was right beside or right under them. Afterwards, the men practiced signal drills, and then mounted and unmounted arms practice.

After that hard day of drilling, caring for the horses still had to be done. Finally, it was chow time. The soldiers were eating when a lieutenant walked into the mess hall. Everyone stood up and were at attention when the lieutenant began to speak.

"Men," he said, "I have an announcement. The commander is calling a full-dress assembly at eighteen hundred hours in the parade field. That is all." He then said, "As you were," and left. The men sat back down and quickly finished their meal before getting ready.

Soon the commander walked onto the parade field. Everyone came to attention as he stood facing his men. The setting sun peered over his shoulder as the red sky, along with the coolness of the early evening, created a peacefulness.

"At ease," the commander said as he glanced around at the rows of men standing before him. He then began his speech. "I am certain many of you have heard the news that fighting has ceased in Europe. An armistice has been signed and adopted by all warring countries. I know that many branches of the service will soon be releasing men early from their military duty. But we all know this cavalry unit is stationed here, on American soil. Our job is not finished. We have a duty to repel any force that may attack or harm America and those who live within its borders.

There is a vast amount of territory that is unsettled along the Mexican border. Because it is so desolate, there is little or no law. And although Mexico's civil war has waned with their signing a new constitution, there are still factions to be dealt with. Until we hear otherwise, the 13th Cavalry will be on duty, and in full force. When your families ask if you are coming home, tell them what you are told. That is all." The commander then turned and walked away.

Arthur knew this news would break his mother's heart. In her recent letter, she was already asking if there was any word of early release. He had to tell her. He went back to his barracks and wrote,

Dear Mama,

I hope this letter finds all of you safe and well. I am sitting here on my bunk tonight, employing my time writing you. I am also sitting here because my butt is so sore from all the time I have spent in the saddle. The men who have been here longer say I will be sore until I get my 'leather butt,' which, I am told, takes better than a month to acquire.

I imagine that you, Albo, and Russell are all working long hours, finishing up the jarring and battening everything down for winter.

I received a letter from Albo a week or so ago, and your letter yesterday. Tell Albo that although I am the eldest son, now, Earl will always be 'Top.'

We were told tonight that the war in Europe is over. Our commanding officer also told us that our job is not finished here, and will not be for the foreseeable future. So, I will not be released early. I understand how you must feel about this Mama, but there is no other choice. Believe me: the moment I do get released; I will be home.

I helped brand the horses the other day. They are branded on their hoofs, so it does not hurt them.

The influenza has become more prevalent here over the last few weeks, but I am fine. I hope it has settled some back home.

Write to me. Tell Albo, Father, and the rest to write also.
Your loving son,
Arthur

Eight days later, he received a letter from his mother.

My little cavalry man,

I am writing this for your Father, also, and he says hello. We were so glad to receive your letter. It came in four days! I hope this letter finds you well and fine. We are all fine here.

Please be careful, my son: do not get the influenza. When you come back someday, you will then notice all the people that are gone because of this plague. And it is still out there. I am so thankful that, although your father, Albert, and I walked through that hospital, we did not come down with it. Lucile and her mother did. But, from the letter Lucile sent, they are both getting better now.

Lucile and her family have moved away. I do not know if it is because of Earl or not. But I do have one regret: I always thought that, because of her background being so different from ours, she would only bring trouble to Earl. I told him that outright, once. After seeing her at his bedside, and then what she wrote in her letter to me, I see I was wrong. I wrote back and told her so. I only wish I could have realized this before Earl was gone.

We bought a nice red granite stone for him—the very best that we could afford. But, still, Mr. Arnold was kind enough to let us make payments on the balance. Lucile had two red geraniums delivered here. She wrote a note, asking if I could plant them at Earl's gravesite. Poor child, I just did not have the heart to tell her that you cannot plant geraniums in November and expect them to live. So, I will keep them here in the house until spring

The other day I went to Earl's grave to sweep the fallen leaves away. When I got there, two perfect, deep crimson roses were neatly laying on top. My first thought was that it had to be Lucile, but that does not make sense. First, she does not live here anymore; and second, why would she send geraniums for me to plant at the wrong time of year if she had visited? I am certain she would have sentenced those plants to a cold death herself.

I know the dark crimson color of those two roses symbolizes something more than what regular red roses do, but why just two? This is something I cannot understand.

The paper shortage from all that has happened has forced us to write short letters, and you well know that we have also had to use scraps of paper to write on, so I am leaving Albert some space to write a few lines below.

Take care my son,

Mother

Hello, old leather butt,

Hope you are doing fine. Just a few words to tell you that since the war ended before I could enlist, I joined the Citizen's Corps instead. We have uniforms and everything. You will know a lot of the members. We train every Thursday in the gymnasium after school lets out. We can even march in formation without falling over each other. I was issued the same 38-caliber handgun that you carry. I practice all the time. I can respectably say that I am now good enough to shoot the fingers off a pollywog at ten paces.

I got a job with old Tazzie Strang, working at his sawmill down by Porky Rocks. It does not pay much, but it's enough that I can get by and still have time to help run the farm.

There was an advertisement I read in the newspaper the other day. It said that the oil companies down in Kentucky have a shortage of experienced tool dressers and they are paying big money to go there. I do not know if I would want to travel that far from home, but you know that I am one of the best tool dressers around. Father taught me well.

Also in the newspaper there was an article that a deer was seen in a field over in Rome Township. There seems to be more accounts of deer sightings all the time. I even heard that the game commission received a railcar load of deer from Michigan and let them go in Forest County. Three were spotted around the Tionesta Hill last week. Maybe someday we will be able to hunt deer the way Grandad did.

Well, all I have to say now is that I miss you, brother, and wish you were here.

Albo

Albert mailed the letter the next morning. It was unseasonably warm and the sun was rising into a perfect blue sky. The sawmill had broken down the day before, so Albert knew he would not have any work.

He walked to the barn to feed the horses. When he looked in on Dolly, she seemed depressed. He decided right then, and grabbed the bridle off the rail hook before opening the stall gate. "Come on girl," he said. "We are going for a ride."

The horse stared at him. Albert felt that, in some strange way, Dolly was waiting for an explanation. He instantly gave one. "I made a deal with Top when I gave him Lucile's card at the pie social. He agreed that I could take you for a ride. So, I am here to collect."

With that speech, he put the bridle on Dolly, led her to the saddle, and strapped it on. He never said goodbye to anyone as Dolly and he strolled out through the open fields in the morning sun and then down the back paths to Pleasantville.

After reaching the other side of town, Albert sensed that Dolly wanted to travel farther. She wanted to run. "All right, girl," he said as he flicked the reins. Dolly instantly launched them. It was just horse and rider as Dolly galloped down the country road as fast as she could go. The sun briskly flickered through the barren trees as the horse's mane twirled. Albert crouched down as the breeze of forward momentum swept his face and fanned his hair. The ride seemed to be running them away from the pain. The horse continued to frolic as they charged farther.

After a time, Albert slowed Dolly to a trot. They then stopped at a creek for the horse to drink. While waiting, Albert closed his eyes and held his face to the sun. The solar warmth seemed to further free him from his grief.

He thought of his older brothers and Jack (but in happier times), and felt the lump in his throat momentarily leave. A smile came to his face as he mounted Dolly, and they traveled on.

Soon they came to a place where Albert had never been. But he'd heard all the stories. It was a city that, at one time, boasted a population of fifteen thousand people. It had been built and then abandoned in less than three years. Pithole's only fault was that it had been a boomtown, built in a time of great excess. Although it had a post office, a train station, over fifty hotels, three churches, and a host of other businesses, the largest share of its population was transient. As oil production quickly declined around Pithole, the land speculators and other itinerant workers left for oil strikes elsewhere. Pithole had been hastily built out of wood, causing it to fall victim to many fires that resulted in tremendous financial losses. Eventually, the few residents who still resided in the city dwindled further, dooming it to become a ghost town.

Albert maneuvered Dolly down what had been streets. After fifty years they were only outlined in the undergrowth, covered by waves of dead grass and weeds. He ducked beneath the occasional branches of young trees and saplings that had taken root.

On each side were remnants of rotting boards (some still nailed together), pieces of crumbling slate roof tiles, rusting corrugated tin, and broken glass and bottles, all protruding from the dead leaves and acting as grave markers for the buildings that once stood there.

Albert thought of all the people whose dreams were crushed by such an exodus. He remembered the stories of the abandoned town being ransacked—of the buildings being scavenged and of whole storefronts being dismantled and taken to other towns.

He finally looked to the sky. The beautiful day was clouding up and it was a long way back. "We'd better go, girl," he said as he pulled on the reins and turned Dolly around.

As they strolled back, it began to sprinkle. Albert pulled his hood over his head and they traveled on.

It was semi-dark when Albert and Dolly reached Pleasantville. The sprinkles had turned into a study drizzle. Albert's head hung low as did Dolly's as they slowly traveled along a side street. They came out from a blind intersection just as a trolley also entered it. The horse shrieked at the site of the trolley and reared straight up. Albert frantically held onto the reins as Dolly lunged for the opposite side of the street. She stumbled on the trolley tracks as her rear hoof lodged into the flangeway space alongside the rail. The horse fell horrifically, brutally launching Albert into the street.

Dolly thrashed and screamed as Albert, dazed and hurt, desperately struggled to his feet. In all of his pain, he limped to the horse. The trolley had pulled up and stopped. Its glaring lights shone through the rain, further revealing the flailing animal. "Dolly! Dolly!" Albert screamed as he dodged back and forth, trying to grab the reins. But Dolly's thrashing was too violent. Just then Mr. Brown, the livery stable owner, ran over. He grabbed Albert's shoulder and pulled him back.

"Son, quit. It is hopeless."

Albert looked as Brown pointed to Dolly's rear leg. It was still lodged in the track, and broken so badly that bone was protruding through the skin.

Albert frantically pleaded, "You can fix her, right? Please! I will pay anything!"

Brown slowly shook his head and solemnly responded, "Son, no one can fix a break like that. . . We cannot let this animal suffer. I will go get my gun."

Albert's heart sank as reality set in. He looked at Dolly, who had settled some due to exhaustion and pain. A crowd gathered as Albert stood motionless, never recognizing their presence. It seemed as if only seconds had passed before Mr. Brown returned. The crowd stepped back as he raised the gun. That was when Albert stopped him. He looked at Brown and said, "I must do this."

Brown saw the distress in Albert's eyes and lowered his weapon. He then handed it to Albert, who took the rifle and reluctantly raised it. Dolly looked straight at him as tears and rain clouded Albert's vision. He could barely see down the sight before he closed his eyes and pulled the trigger. *Boom!* The gun fired.

"No!!!" Albert screamed as he dropped the weapon and collapsed to his knees. With his hands over his face, he trembled in uncontrolled grief.

Brown picked up the rifle, then helped Albert to his feet. Albert wiped his eyes with his rain-soaked sleeve as Brown said, "I will take care of the rest of this, son. Let me get someone to take you home."

"Thank you . . . but, I need to be alone."

"I understand." Brown said as he lightly patted Albert on the shoulder.

Albert turned from the illuminated scene and disappeared into the drizzling night. As he walked, the only sound was the tapping raindrops on the dead leaves. His tears, more than the rain, ran down his face as he made his way home. When he opened the house door, Ella instantly noticed the distress on his face.

"What happened, child?" She asked in a panicked tone.

Albert could only wave his hand as he sat down. Ella gave him the time that he needed and went to gather some dry clothes for him.

As Albert changed, he relayed the story. Ella listened intently as she tended to his cuts and abrasions. She then sat down and cradled him as if he were still a child.

Albert finally muttered, "It seems as if God is punishing us."

"Never say that, child!" Ella scolded. "We do not know why these things happen, and there are other families that are suffering far more."

Albert sat quiet for a moment and then said, "The only comfort I take in this, is that perhaps Dolly and Earl are riding together now."

CHAPTER 26

Patrol, and Leaving for a Job

December 1918 / January 1919

A rthur had been attached to the 13th Cavalry for months. The drills and training were becoming second nature, yet he soldiered on, taking his training to heights of perfection.

It was a Tuesday morning, and the cavalrymen were saddling their horses for morning drills. A newcomer next to Arthur was having problems. The recruit finally felt he had accomplished the saddling task and walked his horse out to the parade field. Arthur followed. As the two lined up at the end of the row, the sergeant shouted, "Prepare to mount!" Everyone stuck his left foot into their horse's stirrup and then stood erect with their knee pressed against the horse's ribs.

"Mount."

In unison, the line of cavalrymen stepped up on their stirrup and threw their right leg over to the other side of the saddle. That is, all except the recruit. He had not tightened the cinch strap properly and the saddle spun, tossing him, butt first, to the ground. Laughter erupted as Arthur jumped from his horse to lift up the recruit.

"Private Ames!" the sergeant shouted. "No one told you to dismount!"

"Yes, sir," Arthur answered as he froze.

"Well?" the sergeant questioned.

Arthur looked at the officer with a puzzled expression.

"Help that man with his saddle!"

"Yes sir!"

Arthur hurriedly ran to the left side of the horse and then, along with the recruit on the right side, they lifted the saddle to its upright position and tightened the cinch strap correctly. The recruit was mounting just as Arthur stepped behind the horse to return to his mount. The horse kicked, launching Arthur in the air before he hit the ground.

The whole cavalry, including the recruit he had just helped, and the sergeant, broke out in uncontrolled laughter.

Arthur, picked himself up, hobbled to his horse, and mounted.

"Private Ames, since you seem to be the entertainment for the day, I will have you demonstrate to our new recruits our balance training drill 'shirt off, shirt on.'"

"Yes sir!" Arthur immediately flipped the reins, and he and his horse shot off at a full gallop around the bullpen ring. With the horse running full speed, Arthur unbuttoned his shirt, pulled it over his head, then held his arms out straight with the shirt in one hand. For Arthur, this was the one drill that he loved. It made him feel like he was flying. He closed his eyes as he and his horse charged around the ring. After two laps, he pulled his shirt back over his head and buttoned it again. He then brought the horse down to a walk before taking his place in line.

The rest of the day was filled with mounted arms training. To fire a gun accurately from a moving horse was a challenge. Not to mistakenly shoot the animal in the back of the head or hit a fellow cavalryman was far more important. Dismounted arms training was easier and safer, and the unit trained that way more often.

In the evening, mail call came. Arthur received a letter from his mother.

My dear son,

I hope this letter finds you well and fine. We are all well here, but the Influenza is roaring its ugly head again. The paper is filling with stories of those who are sick, along with the obituaries of those who have died.

Lee Bills just got home from France. His family is so happy. But Vern Kightlinger has been sent with the occupation army to Germany. His mother has no idea how many months or years he may be gone. Lenard Nason was gassed at one of those battles last July. He is still in some camp hospital.

I must tell you now that Albert was riding Dolly and she got spooked by the trolley and rushed across the tracks. She got her hoof caught in the rail slot and broke her leg. She could not be saved. It has been hard enough on Albert to deal with the loss of Earl and you being gone. Losing Dolly has only added to his pain. He is about to take a tool dresser job with some oil company in Kentucky. I know it pays twice as much as around here, but it breaks my heart to think that I will see another of my sons leave.

If every dark cloud has a silver lining, well, I am still waiting for my silver. Please write to Albert. Tell him not to go.

Take good care of my Artie,

Your loving mother

Arthur immediately wrote. After the big brother talk to persuade Albert not to go, Arthur also included the story of being kicked by the horse. Nine days later, he received a letter back from Albert.

Dear hop-a-long leather butt,

Now that you have received further instruction in 'where the horse wags its tail,' I hope you are walking straight again. At the rate you are going, you should be home real soon just to heal up.

Well, Artie, Mama told me what she had asked of you— but she, and you, did not know that I had already accepted the job down south. In preparation, I also resigned from the Citizen's Corps and turned in my uniform and handgun.

By the time you receive this letter, I will already be doing what you described as 'breathing in my share of coal smoke' from a moving train.

I am headed to some little place just west of Beattyville, Kentucky. They need tool dressers there. Not many men in that part of the country know how to do what father taught me so young. The company is going to pay me eight dollars a day plus room and board, but that will be in the company bunkhouse shanty.

I will not only do tool dressing, but will also be teaching. I figure my first months' pay alone will be enough to buy another horse for Mama and Father.

Well, Artie, I will write you with my address once I get there and am settled in.

I miss you, brother.
Albo

The next day the whole cavalry was informed that soon they would be heading out on patrol. That evening, Arthur struck up a conversation with Matson, an old mule skinner who had been with the thirteenth for years. "There is a fair amount of trouble out there," Matson said. "I remember that, not more than two years ago, I had just been assigned duty with the thirteenth when we got into some fierce skirmishes. We took part in the Punitive Expedition led by old Colonel 'Blackjack' Persing, although you never called him 'Blackjack' to his face, unless you cared to pull latrine duty for the rest of your enlistment. He led us hundreds of miles into Mexico, chasing Poncho Villa. That created quite a ruckus. We shot a lot of Villa's men, but then we got into a battle with the Constitutionalist forces of the Mexican revolution. That almost started a war, and Villa still got away. That all happened before Persing was sent to France to lead our boys over there.

Now, heed my words, Artie. When we go on patrol, do not let the long hours in the saddle lull you into dropping your guard. Keep your wits. Anything can happen out there. I have seen many good cavalrymen, and a few friends, not come back."

Matson then went on to tell of earlier times. He repeated stories told to him by his grandfather, who had told Matson about the

Comanche, the "Lords of the Plains." The Comanche would travel down through Texas, sometimes stopping for water at Las Moras Springs, near Fort Clark, before moving on across the Rio Grande to foray for Mustangs in Mexico.

Arthur listened intently to Matson's stories. Later that evening, he wrote to tell his mother,

Dear Mama and everyone,

I hope all of you are well and fine. I am fine, here. I want to tell you that Albo wrote back to me. He said he would already be gone from home by the time I received his letter. I tried Mama, but Albo had already made up his mind. He is strong and smart, though. He will be fine; so do not worry.

I must tell you that we are going out on patrol along the border. We leave in a few days and will travel from Brownsville to Fort Ringgold, then on to Fort Clark. Altogether, the trip will take around 26 days or so, and we will cover around 360 miles.

The mail will be delayed because of the territory that we will be traveling in. Much of it is desolate and unsettled. So, do not worry if you do not hear from me for a while. I will not be alone. I will be traveling with three hundred fellow cavalrymen and twenty-six Texas Rangers. Write to me as always: your letters will reach me at Fort Clark.

With love,

your son, Artie

Friday came. The 13th Cavalry was aligned in columns. The wagons followed behind and the Texas Rangers brought up the rear.

The command was given, "Walk, march!," and the unit began to move. Stretched out over hundreds of yards, it was a stunning sight of man, animal, and wagons, all moving in unison.

Having been raised in the backwoods, it was especially amazing to Arthur. He imagined that his grandfathers, both cavalrymen during the civil war, would have experienced the same emotional moment.

The troop left Fort Ringgold and soon was traveling along the Rio Grande. Arthur was mesmerized by the desolate beauty of the river on his left and the ruggedness of the brush country on his right. From time to time, the troop would pass a shack or even a small village, but the land was mostly deserted. Come evening of each day, they would make camp. The next morning the journey would begin again, just like the day before.

They had now been on patrol for 13 days, having traveled 24 miles the day before. The Skirmishers had been sent ahead to scout the area and were now just rejoining the main body of the cavalry. Arthur slouched in his saddle just like the other cavalrymen, weary from a journey which still had two weeks or more to go.

The only noise in the heat of midday was that of the hoofs of the horses clomping on the rugged trail and the squawks of the leather saddle.

Boom! Boom! Boom! Boom!

"Scatter!" the lieutenant screamed. Cavalrymen yanked their horses in all directions. The whole unit followed suit.

"Halt down!" Arthur yanked the reins and the horse reared to a stop. He grabbed his rifle and dropped belly-first to the ground.

He lay flat, his gun cocked and pointed in the direction from where the shots had come. A gentle breeze passed by as silence eerily intruded on the tense moment. Arthur looked forward and saw a horse lying on its side. A cavalryman was laying on the ground nearby, moaning.

A captain jumped on his horse and shouted, "Skirmishers! Mount!" He then threw his arm forward to charge. Arthur, along with the rest of the Skirmishers, jumped onto their horses. Arthur flipped the reins hard, and his mount raced off at full speed. The thunderous sound of forty charging horses could not drown out the barrage of gunfire that erupted from behind. Arthur crouched lower in the saddle as the front brim of his hat flipped up from the rushing breeze. His horse seemed to sense the graveness of the situation and further quickened their pace. The squadron raced down the trail at full gallop before the captain gave a hand signal and cut left, off the trail—the Skirmishers followed. They made their way through the mesquite and blackbrush.

Arthur's mind raced. *Are we charging into an army of bandits? Or a couple of fools taking potshots?* Just then: *Boom! Boom! Boom!* Shots rang out again!

"Dismount! Take cover!" the captain yelled as the troopers jumped from their mounts, ground-tying the animals as they ran forward to take cover. Arthur surmised that the Rangers would have charged off to flank the right side. The main cavalry body would soon forge their way up the middle. Suddenly, came the command "Fire!"

Forty guns began firing! *What are we shooting at?* Arthur's mind raced. Suddenly, he caught sight of a figure skulking in the brush. He aimed his gun ahead of the silhouette, just like leading squirrels back home. As the culprit stepped into his sights, he pulled the trigger. *Boom!* The bandit jumped, but did not fall. Surprise caught Arthur. There was no way he could have missed. His bullet must have hit some brush and fragmented. The bandit threw a shot back as he disappeared into the undergrowth.

Out of the corner of his eye, Arthur glimpsed hundreds of cavalrymen climbing through the brush on foot. The shooting intensified. Gunfire erupted on the other flank; the culprits must have run toward the Rangers. After some time, the shooting started to quiet. The captain shouted. "Cease fire! Mount!" And then he commanded, "Forward!"

With guns drawn, the squadron trampled through the brush until they came to a clearing. Three saddled horses stood grazing. Everyone spied the hoofprints of more than a dozen other horses leading away from the fight. They followed in hot pursuit. Suddenly, ahead, gunfire broke out again. The Skirmishers charged toward the sound until they came to the trail along the Rio Grande once more. The Texas Rangers were bunched up ahead. As the squadron reached the Rangers, everyone could see a body floating in the river, and hoof tracks leading up the bank on the other side. Mexico was over there. The cavalry had been ordered not to enter Mexico.

The captain then gave command and the Skirmishers moved on, assuming a vanguard position. They scouted for miles before rejoining the main body at dark.

After all of the action, the rest of the journey was peaceful and the cavalry reached Fort Clark two weeks later.

CHAPTER 27
Homecoming

February thru June 1919

A week of sleeping in a bunk on a mattress and not sitting in a saddle made Arthur and the other men feel better. That patrol had been his graduation to becoming a true leather butt.

The following days turned into weeks as the cavalrymen returned to their mundane duties of taking care of the horses, the barracks, and training. The only excitement was when the Skirmishers were called out to help the Texas Rangers hunt down and recapture two prisoners who had escaped. Just after that episode, Arthur began his basic leadership course, hoping to be promoted to corporal.

During the next month, men began taking sick throughout the fort. More and more were reporting to the infirmary. Arthur himself had developed a persistent cough. He did not dare write home and tell his mother. She would become hysterical at just the mention of sickness. Besides, he would get better soon.

A few days later the fever started, then a headache so debilitating that his eyesight became hazy. He reported to the infirmary and spent days there, along with the others who were terribly sick. His mail piled up. He was too sick to read. Aspirin was given constantly and ice packs were on many foreheads, but the fever became critical. The sick were stripped down to their skivvies. A wet, thin sheet was then laid over them before they were wheeled outside onto the veranda. They were left there through the night. As Arthur shivered, he felt the cold would kill him before the fever.

Arthur became delirious for days until his fever finally broke. It would take more time before he could function or resume duty, but he had gained enough strength to choose a random letter and open it.

My dear little cavalryman,

Received your card. We are all fine, at present. I hope this letter finds you well and fine. Some good news, for once: Romey is back and is well and fine, though someone ransacked his hotel room when he had a layover and stole all his money and clothes. He came home flat broke, with nothing but the clothes on his back. But you know old Romey: nothing has changed him; he just took it all in stride. I have never seen your grandmother so happy before. Some of the stress and worry has now ended, since my brother is home. Now I just need you and Albert back here.

Jackie Litzinger has also gotten home. He has many stories. He spent seven months in that hospital in France. He limps badly and his left arm hangs, but he says he will heal up just fine. Seeing his injuries, I hope and pray that he will.

I must close, now. Before I do, I have enclosed some petals from the blue and pink rambler plant that grows alongside the house. Clara pressed them last fall. We felt they will bring a little of home to you.

With love, Mother

Arthur then spied a letter from Albert, and opened it.

Hello scout,

Mama wrote to tell me you were out sightseeing along the Rio Grande. Well, I guess you did not get my last letter because I have not heard from you. So, I found a big piece of paper and am going to write you a whole book. It will probably cost me half a dollar just to mail it.

Let me tell you about my adventures. I ended up working

just outside of a little town called Irvin, in Kentucky, for a Mr. Dordey. The first well I worked on was along Cow Creek. He was amazed at how fast that well went in. He could not believe that someone as young as I knew more about drilling and tool dressing than his older men. I told him that my brothers and I grew up in the business and our father began teaching us at age twelve. So he made me foreman, and I was training his men.

Everything was fine until the gang I was working with found out how much I was being paid. I had just got my money from the paymaster when three of them approached me. They said that no Yankee was coming down here and being paid more than them. They suggested that I give them half of my money. Well, I told them I did not like that suggestion, so they came at me. We had a regular knock-down fight.

All I can say is that all that bare-knuckle fist fighting paid off. I pulled 'the bug' on the first one. I punched him in the side, and he bent over. When he stood up, I took him right in the jaw. He flew into the creek. All the while, the other one was punching on me from behind. So I spun around and rabbit-punched him so many times that he fell in the water, too. The third guy hesitated, but I kind of liked him. So I just slapped him down.

Next thing I knew, I heard a noise from behind and turned around. There stood two more of them, with a couple powder wagons leveled at me. (Note: slang for a bore-loaded flintlock rifle) They ordered me to get my things and leave. Well, I felt I had worn out my welcome, so I obliged them.

I could have easily gotten another job in Kentucky, but I decided that I should go home where I belong. I feel Top also would want me to.

On another note: maybe Mama has already written you to say that Jim Cross and Bessie Stroup are married. So, if you are still sweet on her, you are out of luck. You need to get home before all the good ones get married off. By the time you get this letter, I may already be home, and I am going hunting.

Albo

He then opened one more.

Dear son,

I have not heard from you in weeks. I am at my wits end. I pray to God that you are all right. Please contact me.

Your loving mother

Arthur, though weak and miserable, found the strength to find a pencil and paper and wrote his mother. He lied to keep her from worrying. He told her he was completely recovered, now. He did get better over the following week, though, and resumed his duties. Afterward, he received a letter back from Ella scolding him for leaving her to worry so long. She then forgave him.

It was a month later, and Arthur was brushing his horse when the sergeant came up to him and said, "Private Ames, the lieutenant wants to see you."

Arthur was puzzled, but followed orders and was soon standing before the lieutenant.

"Private Ames," the lieutenant said, "because of a lack of time, I will get right down to what I have to say. The Thirteenth has been ordered to lower its roster. Your name is on the list for early discharge.

"But I must say that this troop is offering, to the best men on that list, the opportunity to stay by reenlisting now."

Arthur's mind raced, but his heart already knew the answer. "I greatly appreciate the opportunity, sir. But my family needs me."

The paperwork took a few days. Arthur elected to not write home. His mother would be paranoid over his traveling alone, because of Romey being robbed.

Arthur was in dress uniform the morning he was to depart. He turned and waved to his friends, who waved back. He then saluted them just before boarding the Liberty Truck that took him to the train station.

As the train began the long journey home, Arthur stared out the window and reflected on how happy his family and he had been before a great war and a devastating influenza had changed their lives—and, for that matter, the lives of so many millions of people in the world.

He thought of his brother and the smile that Earl would always flash. It was seared into Arthur's memories, along with all the things they had done together … especially that day five years earlier, when they were hunting and the nitro magazine exploded.

He also knew the family would pick up the pieces and return to happiness once more because Earl would be right there, in everyone's heart.

Clara was out front of the house, on her knees, weeding the flower bed behind the picket fence. She was entranced in her work and failed to notice a man walking down the middle of the road. Suddenly she sensed someone's presence and looked through the pickets of the fence. She spied him—someone dressed in uniform with a bag thrown over his shoulder. *He must be a soldier,* she assumed, before resuming her task. Her subconsciousness finally prodded her to look again. She stood and stared.

"Mama!" she screamed as she ran to Arthur and jumped into his arms. Ella and Almon charged out the door in response to Clara's scream. Albert and Russell came running from the barn. In unison, they all saw Arthur holding Clara, and ran to him. A great reunion took place in the middle of that dirt road. The last son was home.

CHAPTER 28
Healing

Mid-June 1919

An automobile pulled up the cemetery's drive and stopped. Its door squeaked open and then quietly closed. A stylish young woman walked to the grave and stood. She stared for the longest time before closing her eyes and taking a deep breath. It was almost summer, yet the air smelled as sweet and fresh as early spring. She noticed the two-tone call of a chickadee, accompanied by the gentle rustling of tree leaves in the faint breeze that caressed her face. She seemed to sense his presence, and opened her eyes. An amazing array of natural beauty surrounded her, but she stood alone.

Lucile's mind retraced time to the pie social, when he had given her that theatrical description of Goodwill Hill. She had questioned him, saying that what he described could be found in many places. At that very moment he said, "Yes." She now understood. It was not one place he was referring to … it was an awareness of nature—something he held dear, unlike so many others.

Although she was bound by rationality, the breeze and the call of the chickadee comforted her. The grief and loneliness she felt, was caused by separation and longing. His love for her was never-ending. The very moment she had laid eyes on him in that classroom, she knew. But the different lives they led caused her to resist his affections. Through time she came to realize that their love could not be denied. It was something deeper, something more, something seldom found. Earl knew. He had told her in his letter when he referred to, "a place beyond the heart."

The piano melody he had played to her, "The Girl with the

Flaxen Hair," haunted her mind as she knelt, took the two crimson roses she held in her hand, and as she had done before, gently placed them on his grave. Only she knew that the blooms not only expressed the deepest sorrow for someone so dearly loved, but also the two years she had known him . . . two years that should have extended into a lifetime. Her eyes welled with tears as her mind said, *I would have gladly lived in that old house. I would give anything.*

After a time, she stood and walked away. For years afterward, just before summer, two deep crimson roses would appear on Earl's grave.

The End

Notes

Almon and Ella were married for fifty years. Ella died on the day of their golden wedding anniversary, October 14, 1944. Almon lived on to personally know many of us great-grandchildren. He died in 1959.

Arthur married Minnie Wright, a girl with silver-blue eyes. They had three children. Their first child (and only son), they named Earl. My father followed in the footsteps of his namesake, working common-place occupations while playing numerous instruments and entertaining people throughout the region for decades. Dad was still playing his trombone for the people at the Oakwood Heights Nursing Home until two weeks before his death at age 95.

Albert married Grace Metzgar. They had nine children. Grace passed away after 38 years of marriage. In 1962, Albert remarried to Beulla Anthony. Albert was two weeks from his 90th birthday when he passed away.

Russell married Mildred Kerr. They had a son. Russell died at age 88. Lingering complications from a motorcycle accident was a factor in his death.

Clara married Claude Stearns. They had a daughter. Clara passed away at age 77.

Jerome "Romey" McCammon never married. He lived the rest of his life on the family farm and died at the age of 49.

John "Jack" Litzinger married and had a family. He stayed close to the Ames family throughout his life and died at age 75. Russell Ames was a pallbearer at his funeral.

Jack is honorarily mentioned in a list of Ames family names.

Five years after losing Earl, Lucile did marry. Life compelled her to move forward. The earlier episode of Lucile's life made her an older bride for her time in history.

Earl Leslie Ames vigorously lived his 23 years of life. He was up before the sun and laid his head down late at night. He ran his farm, operated three oil leases, and gave piano and trombone lessons. He played in the Pleasantville Band, the Grange Symphony Orchestra, and the I.O.O.F. Band. He volunteered his time to play at three different churches and at many patriotic events. Upon his enlistment, Earl played at numerous events in Pittsburgh, including Carnegie Hall, as a member of the Student Army Training Corps Band.

After learning this story from the pictures, journals, letters, postcards, newspaper clippings, and the tribute to Earl, published in the Titusville Herald shortly after his death. I feel I now understand what my Grandad Arthur meant when he once said of his older brother, "Earl was something more." I can only assume that my grandparents' reluctance to talk about the past may have stemmed from a desire not to stir the ashes that would echo memories of such a hurtful time.

Earl's name appears on the World War One Memorials of both Venango and Warren Counties.

About the Author

Ron Allen Ames is a history enthusiast who attributes his 46 years of life experience as a hands-on business co-owner, for giving him insight into human nature, a benefit when portraying the lives of others. The information he received, dating1914 to 1919 is what prompted Ames to bring this history to light in 'An Echo of Ashes.' Ames lives with his wife Cathy in Pennsylvania. They have two grown sons.

Other books previously written by Ron Allen Ames:

'Vessels of the Strand,' a work recognized by Captain Robert Jornlin of the USS LST 325. Through a storyline, this book is derived from letters written home by the Author's father who was stationed on a tank landing ship (USS LST 246) in the Asiatic-Pacific Theater during World War Two. The LST 246 earned 6 battle stars.

'Metal Horses,' a narrative that touches on the sociocultural implications of the muscle car era, and through story, tells of how those cars were actually driven and street raced in the early 1970s.

From Ron:

"I don't see myself as the author of this book, but more of a conduit relaying the information given to me about the past. The family letters, postcards, journals, newspaper articles, and photographs found in a tattered old box contain a record of a somewhat forgotten time when a great war and a pandemic simultaneously struck the world. History records major events, statistics, details of destruction, and world changes, but it often overlooks the home front and the emotional impact of such a perilous time. *An Echo of Ashes* is just one of many stories from this era."

Background Information

An Echo of Ashes is set in the years 1914 to1919, with a significant focus on the pivotal year of 1918. Inspired by information willed to the author, this book vividly brings history to life through its storyline that weaves through actual events.

World War One broke out in Europe in1914, America did not officially enter the war until April 6, 1917. The Spanish Influenza began its devastation in 1918. The simultaneous occurrence of these two cataclysms profoundly affected nearly every aspect of life.

Courtship and marriage were immensely affected by the swift changing events. The closure of social venues such as churches, schools, movie theaters, and other gathering places were meant to curb the spread of the disease, but also created a form of social isolation.

An Echo of Ashes follows the information it was derived from, which put Lucile and Earl's romance beginning before the closure of social venues.

It is of my opinion that it was not only class difference that weighed on Lucile, but also the real fear many young people held at this time of losing a potential spouse to either the war or the influenza. Marriage rates plummeted as many brides-to-be waited, hoping their betrothed would return from duty and that they both would survive the influenza.

Families lost their income earners as husbands, fathers, and sons were drafted, or enlisted. Shell Shock (PTSD) was recurrent among returning soldiers. A spouse dying or being crippled in the war, or either or both spouses succumbing to the influenza caused massive hardship. Shortages of essentials, from sugar to writing paper, restrictions on train travel, and sudden price increases only added to the struggle.

Worldwide death estimates from the Spanish Influenza range from a low of 17 million to a high of 100 million. In America, the influenza claimed approximately 675,000 lives. Pennsylvania bore the brunt of the pandemic, recording the highest death toll of any state in the union. October 1918 was the deadliest month for America in both the war and the pandemic. Newspapers often listed local Spanish Flu victims on one page, while another page would list local servicemen who had died, were wounded, or were missing in action.

www.statista.com/statistics/1103622/mortality-rate-per-us-state-spanish-flu/

When the American Expeditionary Forces first landed overseas, they were held behind the front lines for further training in specific warfare tactics. Initially, American soldiers were somewhat ill-equipped for this kind of combat compared to their European counterparts who had already been fighting for nearly three years. The first American soldiers wore only cloth insignia hats. England supplied metal helmets until America could produce its own.

Significant advances in armaments led to mass casualties for all sides. Despite the tremendous bravery of those facing the guns in France, 9 to 11 million military personnel died on all sides. Including civilian casualties, the death toll reached 15 to 22 million. Approximately 116,500 Americans lost their lives, including over 400 American women who died overseas in various supporting roles from nursing to telephone operators.

A large share of America's casualties occurred in the last year of the war with over 26,000 American soldiers dying in just 47 days of fighting during the Meuse-Argonne Offensive. An Echo of Ashes offers a glimpse into what Jack could have experienced in this battle.

Around 30,000 World War One American soldiers lie buried in Europe, and 4,400 remain listed as missing in action.

www.nps.gov/wwim/wwioverview.htm

www.worthpoint.com/dictionary/p/militaria-weapons/us-world-war-i/headgear-united-states-world-war-one

www.worldwar1centennial.org/index.php/communicate/press-media/wwi-centennial-news/1168-u-s-female-casualties-of-world-war-i.html

Telegrams were infrequently used during World War I due to the high cost, leaving letters and postcards as the main correspondence venue. Soldiers overseas were not required to use postage. Instead, they wrote 'soldier mail' where the stamp would go. Sensors read all mail and removed anything detrimental to the war effort. Only then was the envelope given a round blue ink stamp and allowed to pass on to loved ones and friends. With a vast number of Americans away from home, a writing paper shortage developed in some areas. Many people resorted to using any kind of scrap paper available to write on. Frequently, the pages, and the envelopes held messages from multiple people. At times every open space on the paper was used, including around the outside edges.

War Letters: Communication between Front and Home Front

Imagine a world without cellphones, TV, computers, email, texting, social media, the internet, telephones, or radio. Most rural areas were without electricity at this time in history. Manual labor made up the bulk of the work available. People in the countryside would rise with the dawn and spend the daylight hours working. For many, the workday ended with sunset. Evenings were spent by candle or lantern light. Common personal activities included reading, music, journaling, letter writing, crafts, and singing. Sundays were social days, often including church and other gatherings. Learning to play a musical instrument was common. Earl (Top) was an exemplary trombonist and pianist. His talent provided the opportunity for him to know Lucile. Although not mentioned in the book, information shows that Earl was also proficient with the trumpet and violin.

An Echo of Ashes touches on the dangers of oil production and how an average Pennsylvania oil lease operated in the 1900s. Earl was unique in that he employed his horse Dolly in his tasks of operating oil leases, while the majority of lease operators at this time traveled on foot.

Oil changed the world into what it is today. Oil is not only used to make fuel for our vehicles but also medical drugs, cosmetics, plastics, many of the colors we see, lubricants, waxes, solvents, asphalt for roads, synthetic fibers for clothing, floor coverings, tires, and a host of other products.

Oil saved the whales, as whale oil was the primary source for lamp fuel before kerosene, made from oil, became common.

All of this is possible because of a group of visionaries led by Colonel Edwin Drake, who developed the first successful oil well in 1859, just outside of Titusville, in Northwestern Pennsylvania. Oil exploration spread across the country and then the world. Oil and the products derived from it will always be a part of our modern-day lives. To learn more about oil and its history, visit:

www.drakewell.org

The Mexican Revolution started in 1910. America reinforced its border with Mexico in 1911. The build-up included the US 13th Cavalry along with other cavalry units. The added strength was to protect border towns and America's sovereignty due to the lawless environment in Mexico that could have spilled over onto American soil. America added further forces to the border after the "Zimmerman Telegram," a correspondence sent from Germany to Mexico, proposing a joint alliance to fight the United States. The US 13th Cavalry did not leave the border until 1921.

For military and firearms enthusiasts, in one letter in the book my Great Uncle Albert (Albo) refers to his 38 caliber sidearm as being the same as his brother Arthur's, (Artie) who was in the US 13th Cavalry. I too was confused about this being an army issued sidearm to the rank and file during World War One. The M1911 produced by Colt and Springfield, and the M1917 Smith and Wesson 45 caliber handguns were the most common. After some diligent research the answer is that due to production issues there was a shortage of 45s. The army began to issue the Colt M1892 and M1901, 38 caliber sidearms to those other than higher ranks. Many of these 38s were refurbished, older guns.

www.americanrifleman.org/content/the-springfield-colt-model-1911-hybrid-a-result-of-wwi-production-issues/www.americanrifleman.org/content/america-s-military-revolvers/

World War I and the Spanish Influenza profoundly impacted America. The war created a mix of fear, anticipation, and a sense of patriotism. The influenza brought on helplessness and uncertainty, yet it also fostered in a stronger sense of caring and community. Both events caused widespread economic hardship and anxiety. Many families experienced loss and mourning. The far-reaching impact affected America's social dynamics, politics, and culture for years to come. World War I reshaped America's role in the world. www.neh.gov/humanities/2017/summer/feature/world-war-i-changed-america-and-transformed-its-role-in-international-relations

In conclusion, the generation that endured World War I and the Spanish Influenza are to be revered for their fortitude, perseverance, and sacrifice. Most of their selfless acts remain unrecorded. Of those who lost the most, many moved forward to find hope and happiness again. *An Echo of Ashes* is just one of countless stories from this perilous chapter in history that has somewhat faded into the annals of time.

Music referred to in, *An Echo of Ashes*:

'The Girl with the Flaxen Hair' (piano) by Claude Debussy
'The Star-Spangled Banner' by Francis Scott Key
'Cover Them Over with Beautiful Flowers' by E.F. Stewart
'Battle Cry of Freedom' by George Fredrick Root
'Stomp Off, Let's Go' by Evergreen Classic Jazz Band
'Gymnopedies' (piano) by Erik Satie

'Reverie' (piano) by Claude Debussy
'Mazurka in A Minor, Opus 17, Number 4' (piano) by Frédéric
    Chopin
'My Country, 'Tis of Thee' by Samuel Francis Smith
'America the Beautiful' by Katharine Lee Bates
'Clair de Lune' (piano) by Claude Debussy

Visit www.historiumpress.com